RANSOM

A Rapunzel retelling of strength and honor

RANSOM

A Rapunzel retelling of strength and honor

C. C. SCHMIDT

SWEETWATER
BOOKS

An imprint of Cedar Fort, Inc.
Springville, Utah

ISBN 13: 978-1-4621-3832-6

Published by Sweetwater Books, an imprint of Cedar Fort, Inc.
2373 W. 700 S., Springville, UT, 84663
Distributed by Cedar Fort, Inc., www.cedarfort.com

LIBRARY OF CONGRESS CONTROL NUMBER: 2020938116

Cover design by Wes Wheeler
Cover design © 2020 Cedar Fort, Inc.

Printed in the United States of America

10 9 8 7 6 5 4 3 2 1

Printed on acid-free paper

1

POPPY SEEDS

The creaking of an ancient weathered axle interrupted the serenity of the countryside as two wooden wheels resisted the rough, underused trails. Aged, leathery hands gripped tightly as the man pressed forward, hobbling on his good leg and dragging the disfigured one behind him. His muscles cramped and stiffened from constant jerking. Every other uneven step sent a shooting pain from his hip, yet he pressed on. His withered body refused to cover ground as quickly as it used to, and the slow pace strained his frail frame.

His tattered, dusty apparel and unshaven jaw made him look like a beggar, but under the begrimed appearance was a man with more riches than a czar or king. At any time he could swap the threadbare rags for new, brightly colored apparel, but he didn't want to attract any attention from extravagant clothing. Although his carefully curated merchandise could thwart the picky robber, a hasty, eager thief might not be so fastidious, swiping anything greedy hands could touch. He felt it always best to appear all but invisible.

Trinkets and baubles inside the rickety cart appeared less than desirable—scuffed, aged, and worn—but each and every piece nestled together pulsed with the weighty intrigue of treasure. The relics, unique and heavily used, had long been fortified with infusions of ancient magic, and the old man served as their designated peddler and keeper. Shuffling slowly from town to town, magically guided by the inanimate pieces themselves, he fulfilled his purpose dutifully.

Among the curios, a talisman from across the great sea, carved out of cypress from the swamps of the bayou, slid back and forth. Thin leather straps that once tethered the magic piece around the neck now wound and tangled around fellow dormant relics. Another piece glistened when it caught the sunlight, with intricate golden swirls surrounding a rectangular handheld mirror. Swooping leaves of gold flowed down, forming the handle in the most beautiful manner, ending in a magnificent rose in bloom. Said to show anything to the possessor, the mirror appeared worthlessly clouded with age. Next to it lay a spindle, taken from a spinning wheel burned in a heap of similar frames. It appeared plain to the untrained eye, but the power and sharpness was obvious to those who were looking. Pinging against the deadly needle, a clear jar rolled back and forth on its side, its lid screwed tight. Inside the thick glass a small, swirling storm cloud churned, and if one were to look closely, they would witness never-ending snowfall.

Clattering loudly against large and small wares, an old oil lamp, tarnished and discolored, bounced in the cart as well. A tiny voice usually called out from inside, although the occupant became less chatty during prolonged travel. Long and sleek, dull and rusted, the lamp was the reason for excursion now. Leading by magic in the direction it was meant to go, the peddler dutifully followed. Yes, the distance was far and tiresome, but the reward was always worth the pain. So, he pulled along, just as he had done for a hundred years.

Heading south, the lamp guided its keeper around Mächtig Mountain. Enormously powerful, the mount lay on the southern border of the kingdom of Stillemäch. Impressive snowy peaks dusted the blue sky, seen by all for several days before travelers reached the base of the great mountain. Inclining quickly, dangerously jagged, the foothills forced every road to veer, discouraging all from a foolish attempt over.

Bumping and winding carefully, the peddler regretted the path of choice, pulling across what was no more than a sparse trail, and not a very good one at that. Rocks and thick tufts of grass hampered progress, catching the wooden wheels on the barely visible ruts while tripping feet with the help of sudden earth mounds. Then, without warning, the road vanished, swept away in a vicious mudslide some months before, the earth long since dried to create a gap in the pitiful trail. Sighing heavily, the peddler geared up to blaze through sloping grounds of debris and soft earth. As he pulled, one squeaky wheel banged roughly against a hidden boulder, and the cart lurched wildly. The unexpected obstruction caught him by surprise, and the frail man stumbled wildly to the side. A small pouch hanging across his chest for protection swung from the safe haven of his body, causing a magic poppy seed, the size of a pin prick, to fall from the leather bag without notice.

Moving quickly to prevent the loss of precious cargo, he righted the wheels, regained composure, and straightened the cart before carefully skirting around the obnoxious boulder. His heart raced from the burst of exertion, but despite the chaos, a smug grin bloomed across his dry lips at a job well done.

Left behind, the tiny seed immediately sank into the rich soil, planting powerful magic. Roots spread quickly, reaching out into the colossal mountain, and the long stringy veins not only drank in water but also sucked in the strength of Mächtig. For every inch the enchanted poppy grew, the mountain shrank one thousand feet. Within a short time, the great Mächtig Mountain vanished entirely, leaving behind a beautiful poppy bush, full of giant bright red blooms. The seemingly ordinary flowers stood tall in the grasses, soaking up the sun just as any common bush. But inside the stems, petals, and leaves hid extraordinary power and the strength of a mountain.

Eyes flashed in the darkness as scavengers began their evening routines. Scurrying paws scratched and pattered while the low call of an owl murmured in the early night. Like the shadows of many disproportionate trees lining the lonely road, the Crooked Elm sat skewed and lopsided on the side of the darkened highway, waiting to offer paying travelers pitiful food, adequate drink, and the type of lodging one weighs against sleeping in the mud. Serving as a haven from the rough, lonely trail, nothing impressive stood out with the contorted inn. Even so, any traveler having made it this far happily accepted the accommodations with gratitude deep in their weary bones.

Inside, creaking wooden joints groaned in the empty tavern as only two rooms sat claimed for the night. The crisp sound of cards being shuffled cut through the stale air as an old hunter, withered from age and covered in dust, sat at his favorite table playing alone. The second patron sat heavily, sunken on his stool, head lying on the worn-out bar top while drool spilled from his gaping mouth. Sounds of cloth swooshing against metal constantly interrupted the peace as the large tavern keeper continued his usual work. Obsessively, the man polished semi-clean tankards, working the filthy cloth quickly in and out of each tin cup, somehow leaving them dirtier than before.

Slowly, the iron hinges of the thick wooden door creaked open, and an old man hobbled in with one straight leg and one crooked, making his way to a certain table. Though not the fanciest nor most comfortable place to rest, the Crooked Elm always had an empty bed, no matter when the peddler travelled through.

"Ah, Torban," a loud voice boomed from behind the bar. "My old friend! You've made it back this way." The large man filled a filthy tankard with a frothy amber liquid and pit it down onto the small table in front of his latest customer. "I've been wondering. Didn't know how many trips ye had left in ya," he said, patting the tired man once heartily on the back.

"Yes, yes. I may be slow and crooked, but I still have a spring in my step," the old, bone-tired Torban responded softly.

The tavern keeper huffed a small laugh, but, like a good host, clomped back behind the counter, leaving his patron in peace.

The peddler pulled the satchel from across his chest, as he always did when he stopped for the night, and began counting the tiny black seeds. Puzzlement bloomed across his wrinkled face and he counted again. Usually untroubled by fellow travelers, the strange behavior of the peddler was quite distracting, and soon the old hunter curiously observed a befuddled old man. After watching the peddler count for the fourth time, he lay his cards face down and slid the chair back, slowly lifting himself from the seat. Aged bones cracked from stiffness, forcing the old guy to take his time wandering across the room.

Once standing directly across from Torban, the hunter slicked back stubby gray hair, picked yellowed teeth quickly, and presented his most charming self. "Excuse me, Monsieur. I am most curious. May I inquire as to what you are about? Have you lost something, and may I assist?"

Torban glanced up at the new friend for an instant but went quickly back to counting for a sixth time. "Dear me, dear me. I fear I have lost something. Something of great value."

The hunter studied the tiny seeds and scoffed but attempted to suppress his incredulity. "You've lost a seed?" The words were produced slowly.

"A magic seed!" Torban snapped. Eyes looked up quickly as he realized he'd revealed more than intended, but upon surveying his elderly companion, he determined a man almost as aged as himself would be no problem. "A magic seed," he repeated more calmly and nodded at the chair across the table.

The hunter pulled the chair back and settled in. "What do you mean, 'magic seed'?" he asked with curious eyes.

Torban ignored the eagerness in his new friend's voice, grateful to talk through the befuddlement, and began to share. "Just what I said. Magic seed. These here have been enchanted by a very powerful magic indeed. As the flower grows, the roots pull in the strength from surrounding objects. Those objects minimize, but the flower grows. The trick, though, is that it appears as an ordinary plant, while inside courses strength one-thousand fold."

Soaking in every word, the hunter became increasingly intrigued. "Why would one want such a flower?"

"Power!" Torban blurted out, then took a swig of the drink in front of him. Foam clung to his mustache as he set the tin cup down a little harder than intended. "The power of the enchanted flower can be harnessed through a chant. Imagine strength unparalleled, youth, and eternal life. What could one accomplish with that?"

"A chant? Seems unlikely. What are the words?" The old hunter leaned in, eager to memorize every morsel the peddler was willing to reveal.

Torban took another deep swig, settling a bit. "Oh, you don't want to know all that. The seed is long gone." He waved a withered hand in dismissal.

"Long gone," the man repeated, then hailed the large tavern keeper. "Another for my friend." The barkeeper refilled their tankards, and Torban drank happily. Calculating, the hunter waited a short time, filling it with small talk and bottomless brew. Soon the peddler seemed adequately at ease, and the hunter decided to try his luck once more. "Going back to one of our earlier topics, I just can't get something out of my head. I understand that the missing seed is lost forever, but what would you chant if you had it? It's just so fascinating."

"Fascinating it is, but magic is not to be trifled with," Torban warned without heart, enjoying the break from a solitary existence. "Oh, all right. The chant is a simple one. Now, let's see . . . oh, right! 'Strengthen marrow, strengthen bones. Time reversed, stand all alone. Recover, revive, redeem, renew. Become the person that I once knew.' Yes, that's it!" Torban smiled, clearly proud of his acute memory, aged as it was.

Pushing back slowly, the hunter raised his old body from the chair. "Well, friend, that was a riveting tale. I am truly sorry for your loss. I hope you may one day recover such a rare seed."

"Oh, the seed will never be retrieved," Torban replied off-handedly. "It plants itself instantly, and the flower grows rather quickly. I don't have the time, energy, or space in my cart to backtrack and dig up a bush now. I'm on a very important errand, you know."

"Indeed." The man smirked as he collected his things. "Oh, what kind of flower did you say that was?" he asked in a disinterested manner, catching the peddler mid-drink.

Torban placed his tankard on the table, much calmer than when he first arrived. "Poppy. Red poppies," he muttered.

"Excellent. Good luck to you, friend. Safe travels. I must be on my way." The man walked briskly into the cool night, leaving cards on the table and a room empty. Carrying all he owned on his back, he turned north, excitedly venturing forth on a new hunt.

✳ ✳ ✳

His heart pounded with excitement. He had spent five days carefully walking and meticulously searching, nearly giving up and almost turning back. But finally Draven the hunter spotted the bright red poppies in the distance. Like many others, he had passed through this valley before, but it hadn't been a valley then. *Wasn't there once an enormous mountain in this area, or is that just my old mind playing tricks on me?*

Closing the gap between him and his target, Draven approached the only poppy plant for hundreds of miles. Vibrant red stood out among the wild green grasses, out of place and stunning. "Now, how does this work?" he murmured to himself, excited but cautious. "Pluck the flower and receive the power?" Drawing his knife, Draven sliced the stem of the longest poppy and held the flower reverently in his hand. Caressing the red petals, he recited the words that the peddler mumbled and then waited. One second. Two seconds . . . Twenty. Nothing happened.

"Drat," Draven exclaimed under his breath, "maybe the old goat's out of his mind after all." Dropping the stem, he reached up and touched one of the four remaining flowers and recited the words once again. "Strengthen marrow, strengthen bones. Time reversed, stand all alone. Recover, revive, redeem, renew. Become the person that I once knew."

A sudden rush coursed through his veins like he had never felt before. Power returned to his weary limbs as his worn out back straightened perfectly. Hair on his head and face regained the deep brown lost so long ago, and he watched as the skin on his hands tightened. Light on his feet, Draven felt as if he were in the prime of his life while adrenaline and energy pumped through his veins. For the first time in many years, he knew he could climb, or even run, up a mountain.

"Incredible," he exclaimed, flexing his muscles again and again. "But how long will it last? I can't dig it up, or I might ruin the magic. I can't leave it the way it is either. The poppies are too bright, and anyone could come along and pick them without knowing their value. They must remain hidden." Gathering long branches, he wove a rough dome that could be used to cover the plant, just as he did when creating a blind spot in the forest. The camouflage appeared as a small, wild bush, scraggly and insignificant, completely covering the poppies. Not one bit of red showed. "There. Now no one will ever know this plant is here, and I will live youthful and strong forever."

For several decades, that was just what happened.

2

A QUEEN'S PRINCE

"Make it stop!" she yelled before transitioning to a low, prolonged moan. Sweat dripped down the beautiful face, causing her golden hair to lie flat, matted in wet strands against red cheeks. Big green eyes shut, and fists clenched tight as another attack rolled in. "Ahhhh!" The agonizing scream penetrated the thick stone walls of the castle, floating into the courtyard below. Nearly three days of hard labor and nothing to show. Contractions rolled through the queen's body so close together she hardly had time to catch her breath. Screams were the only release from the torture.

"I'm here, my love. Just breathe. It'll be over soon," King Barrett mumbled as he sat beside his wife, unsure of what to do. Clumsily, he offered sips of water or rubbed her aching back before she slapped his hand away. He had been told that birth was no place for a king, let alone a man, but Barrett would hear none of that and had sat beside her through the entire excruciating experience.

"I need to move," the queen announced, pushing the down duvet to the side. She attempted to stand, hoping to relieve pressure.

Immediately, the physician forced her back on the royal mattress against the mountain of pillows. "Your highness must remain in her bed. It is not proper to wander about in your condition," he said, and then turned to counsel with those waiting to assist, mumbling something incoherent about women not knowing what's best. Panicked, she turned to her husband and tried to say something, but the hurricane deep inside quickly rolled in again, and the pain took over her body.

The scream startled the pompous physician and his assistants, resulting in more monotone mumblings.

When the latest wave receded, Felicity looked at her attending maid. "Go," she nearly whispered. "I need her now." The order was faint but firm. Concerned, the young woman immediately turned, quickly disappearing out the side door of the bedchamber.

King Barrett made a small noise of disapproval. "I don't think that's necessary," but the instant death stare from the love of his life silenced all doubts.

Within less than a minute the maid returned, followed closely by a short, round woman in a simple gray housedress and white apron. The midwife pushed in with an air of authority, immediately taking charge. Sweeping to the queen's side, she began assessing. "You're a little warm, my dear, but that is to be expected." Her hands rested on the swollen belly, prodding gently. "Ah, I feel the little one. Breach. Stay alert, me lady. Ye must remain strong."

"What is *she* doing here?" The physician was both offended and put-out by the unwelcome presence of the midwife. A female who practiced medicine! "Sire, I have everything under control. My assistants are more than capable. We do not require the pathetic pittance of help this ill-trained woman has to offer."

Before the king could answer, the queen dropped all sense of decorum and screamed, "Out!" She pointed to the main chamber door before doubling forward, feeling the storm churning again.

Dumbfounded, the physician looked to his king for intervention but found no vindication. Instead of coming to his aid, King Barrett boomed, "You heard your queen! Out!" With that, Barrett turned his back on the appalled doctor and his team of confused lackeys. They scoffed and tsked audibly as their leader packed his lances and poultices, then led the group out of the royal bedchamber in a huff.

Booming when needed, Barrett could also speak gently when appropriate. "Can you help her?" he asked softly.

The midwife rolled her gray sleeves up without response and continued examining the queen's belly. She felt her pulse, timed the contractions, and checked dilation, just as the physician had done. Instead, however, of using blood letting, the wise midwife pulled from her bag herbs and oils, mixing powdered marjoram with dried clary sage, and adding oil of lavender as well. She rubbed the aromatic mixture in particular places on Felicity's exhausted, swollen body.

"She's weakening." The midwife spoke cautiously. "Her body must relax. The only thing I can think of, at this point, is an elixir that requires a rare flower for these parts. A poppy. It will relax her tense muscles enough to allow the body to proceed. Can that be found?" she asked, rubbing the inner part of the weakening woman's calf muscles.

"Whatever you require, we shall find it. Just save them both. Please." Barrett looked down at his beloved wife with devotion and fear, his eyes beginning to fill. Lifting her hand to his mouth, he planted a gentle kiss, then turned to go before the tears fell. Another violent scream pierced the air as he exited the chamber.

Calling the leaders of the Royal Cavalry, King Barrett issued a command across the entire kingdom of Stillemäch to scour near and far in search of the elusive poppy flower.

With eagerness and intrigue, every available man immediately began the search. Hour after hour, excitement slowly withered, leaving room for doubt as the idea of finding such a rare bloom so quickly seemed futile. The queen continued to fade. Strength drained with every forceful contraction, and her body slowly gave up in response. Pain continued to rip through her body full force, but progress was too minimal for anyone to hold out hope much longer.

Some commoners and peasants began to lose vigor, eventually returning home to their families with shoulders slumped in frustration and head hung in shame. Others, more duty bound and driven by orders, continued to searched the countryside without falter, among which rode a seasoned knight in gleaming armor with his young, eager squire at his side. The pair galloped south, scanning every direction while gaining ground. Soon, the pair entered the mysterious Valley of the Mountain before they were fully aware of their location. The fearless knight, finally recognizing their surroundings, slowed his horse to a walk. The squire slowed as well, his head swiveling with trepidation. "Sire, where are we?" he finally asked with both reverence and curiosity.

Scanning the land, avoided by all due to superstition, the knight spoke quietly, keeping an even tone. "I'm not entirely sure. It can't be Valley of the Mountain, could it? Have we gone that far?" He pulled on the reins, his strong voice wavering slightly. "Let us turn back. Nothing good comes from this place," he added, pulling the stallion around.

"How do you know there's nothing here?" the young squire inquired.

Rolling his eyes, the knight gained a little of his bravado back as he recounted the fables of childhood. "There is nothing here because not even a mountain would stay." His gloves tightened on the leather reins, and the horse halted obediently. Following suit, the squire pulled back and his mare reluctantly obeyed as well. Perched atop their mounts for a moment, soaking in the stillness as they surveyed the land, the knight continued. "They say this valley once possessed a mountain named Mächtig. It was the largest in the world, but one day the mountain decided that this soil was not rich enough, and it moved east. Somewhere beyond the horizon, Mächtig found a new home to settle on, where the land was rich and the rains were plentiful. Ever since, this valley has been cursed. Travelers used to come through here from many parts of the country, but all avoid this area now. Even the . . ."

"Sire! I think I see something," the squire interrupted excitedly.

"See what, lad? There's nothing here but a few scrawny bushes." The knight laughed, gently nudging his horse around to head back.

The young squire remained still, pulling on the reins to keep his own steed from following. "No, sire. Look! I saw a flash of red, I think."

Irritated, the knight glanced back. "Impossible! There's nothing there. Wait!" He cut himself off this time. "I see something. Let's ride!" With a new sense of urgency, the pair galloped forward, kicking up earth in a flurry of hooves.

They covered the short distance quickly, and the two men jumped hastily from their mounts, covering the last bit of ground on foot until they reached the place that had flashed red. A disappointingly homely bush sat among the grasses, and the squire sighed. "I'm sorry, sire. I thought, or maybe I just hoped, that it could be." He lowered his shoulders, trailing off in self-pity.

"Quiet, lad. Look!" the knight hissed, leaning forward. He pointed through the leaves and thickly intertwined branches. Red peeked through bashfully just when the breeze rustled the blanket of leaves. If the two men weren't so determined to find the crimson shade, the tiny glimpses of scarlet would have been easily overlooked, just as they had been by hundreds before.

The squire shut his mouth instantly and bent down to peer through the foliage. "Whoa!"

"Tear these branches down," the knight commanded, readjusting his gloves.

With quick hands, the squire jumped into action, pulling branches, dismantling the blind limb by limb. With his heart racing with anticipation, decorum was thrown aside as the knight jumped in as well, too eager to stand by. In no time, four vibrant red poppies stood tall and proud, surrounded by a wreath of sticks and leaves stripped hastily from their makeshift haven. The squire's chest rose and fell dramatically, his breath heavier than normal as he stood in silence, entranced by the mythical plant.

"We found it," the knight exhaled in breathy reverence. "We found it!" he shouted, patting the lad on the back. Excitement quickly morphed into duty. "Quick, there's no time," the knight barked as he stepped forward, gathered the green stems in one bunch, and braced shiny black boots on the grassy floor. Muscles strained and teeth gritted as he pulled as if his life—or more important the queen's—depended on it, using the full weight of his body. The thick roots clung to the soil underground with all their might, but slowly, one by one, they relented to the persistent man, releasing their hold on the spot that had been home for many, many years.

Roots in their entirety finally left their soil bed, causing the knight to stumble back. Bracing himself, the squire caught the older man, assisting until he was able to steady his feet. Triumphantly, the knight lifted the entire poppy plant high in his grasp with thick, long roots sprinkling a dirt trail. Withering slightly, leaves seemed in shock from their abrupt disturbance, but four blooms remained strong and bold. "Let's ride!" Still in awe, the squire shook himself before he was able to swing into the saddle. Together, the two kicked off at a full gallop toward home. Their bodies tensed as the horses sped off, the beasts exuding the excitement from their riders.

Pacing by the gate, the midwife nervously waited for any news or offering, losing hope with each hour. Every woman of the castle worked tirelessly on the second floor, tending to the queen in her tragic state, and every man was gone, seeking a miracle. Silence fell with the sun, and somberly the midwife knew they would not have a queen come morning. She turned to head back inside when the sound of wild hooves approached like thunder. Before she had time to react, two men burst through the gate. Her tense, fearful face slacked with relief as the knight rushed forward and pushed the plant into her chubby, capable hands.

Without a word, she whisked the plant away, climbing the stairs to the queen's chamber with purpose. Chopped, pulverized, and boiled, the beautiful flower turned into a pungent, bubbling concoction. Every bit of the flower was used: roots, stems, leaves, petals. Taking very little time, but worrying everyone all the same, the midwife finally completed the process and hurriedly carried the elixir to her highness.

Weakening with every contraction, Felicity could not lift herself from the pillows, too weak to endure the complications, and too tired to push. Carefully, the elixir was poured into her limp mouth. Her face scrunched in reaction to the bitterness, and her mouth clamped shut to stop the acrid syrup from sliding down her throat.

"It's all right, me dear," the midwife cooed. "Open yer mouth. If not for you, then for the babe."

Slowly, Felicity relented, first with only a few drops, but with every swallow she was able to take more. Soon, her pallid skin glowed with color, and she raised her head, sat up, and finally stood. Contractions rolled through, one on top of the other, but this time her body progressed the way it was meant to, and soon she was ready.

Within a short time of the queen swallowing the elixir, the healthy wail of a baby boy filled the royal corridors. Muscles finally released their tension, and Queen Felicity rested against her pillows, finally free from the ripping pain. Soft cooing came from the bowed head of the king as Barrett bounced gently, fawning over his son. The midwife tended to the needs of the new mother gently and efficiently, while the maids reached for the infant, trying their best to pry the prince from his father's loving arms. Finally giving in, the king slowly released his careful grip on the tiny boy, allowing the servants to whisk the newcomer from his arms and tend to their work. Instead of watching them bathe the babe, he turned his attention to the woman he loved and, in a few wide strides, crossed the room to be near his wife. Brushing back the wet locks of hair, his lips pressed against her forehead with the passion of one who helplessly stood by as all had almost been lost. For a moment he believed that his life had forever changed into something unbearable, but that drink, that poppy concoction, had brought Barrett's wife back to him and had given him a son he had already said goodbye to.

"You did good," he whispered, a smile peeking through his chestnut beard.

Weakly, she reached up and brushed back a rogue brown strand off his forehead. "That was awful," she replied simply, then relaxed into a deep, bone-weary sleep.

3

THE LOST LIFE

News of Queen Felicity's near-death experience and the birth of the prince spread like wildfire throughout the kingdom. The evening was alive with tales passing from customer to merchant, soldier to captain, valet to maid, and by morning the entire kingdom of Stillemäch was vibrating with the exciting tale. A constant buzz hummed through the streets as commoners casually passed along speculative ideas of what had happened, the townsfolk making up wild tales to satisfy their thirst for drama until lords and ladies were able to spread their hard earned details. Every nobleman vied for a chance to congratulate the king, which he graciously accepted with misty blue eyes. Every noblewoman attempted to enter the royal bedchamber for a chance to visit the queen and be the first to see the baby, but their royal highness ordered the chamber doors closed to all except her attending midwife, maid, and husband.

"So many noble ladies out yer door, yer majesty." The round midwife made conversation as she checked the queen from head to toe. "They're going to bust down that barrier of yours if ye don't let them have a quick peek soon."

Slowly, Felicity raised herself to a sitting position, relying heavily on all the pillows for support. She brushed her blonde hair out of her eyes, the strands flowing back straight as straw, falling over her shoulder in a golden waterfall. Though exhausted, her eyes lit up with humor. "Let them fret. I'd love to see the ladies of court try to break the door, actually. I've been needing some entertainment."

"Yes, yes, entertaining indeed, but the young master wouldn't much care for that, now would he?" the busy midwife stated matter-of-factly as she nodded toward the extravagant bassinet in the corner under the windowsill. There, swaddled in the warmth of finely woven linens, lay the most perfect little prince.

"No, I suppose he wouldn't," Felicity agreed with a sigh, her face immediately lighting with a warm, motherly smile. "I was afraid he'd never get here."

"We were all afraid," the midwife responded, bustling about, emptying pots and folding linens. "But you're here, and he's here, and that's all that matters. So, when are ye gonna show those ladies this wee strapping lad?"

The queen huffed, "Let them wait. This baby is not just their prince, he's everyone's. They can see him for the first time alongside the entire kingdom tomorrow when we present him properly. Until then, I just want this boy all to myself for one more night."

The heart of the city beat strong as hundreds flowed in and out of the daily market. Draven held his breath while walking past the wool merchant, skeins laid out, freshly cleaned. Merchandise was thick and well sheered, but the odor was unpleasantly pungent. Next to the wool, a man sat with an exhaustive number of barrels containing spices, some familiar, most unknown. The scent in the air adjusted with every step, changing from earthy to sweet, and then a spice reached his nostrils. "Achoo!"

"White pepper, sir. Would you care to try?" the merchant offered eagerly.

Draven wiped his nose quickly. "No! Anything that potent can't be safe to consume." Mumbling a few more choice words, he continued perusing before a crowd caught his eye. Many gathered around a fruit stand in the middle of the square, listening to a boisterous knight speaking animatedly in the center. Curious, Draven made his way over, pushing through to hear what tale had captured the attention of so many.

"I looked across the valley, so dead and desolate. We were near dehydrated. My squire said to me that he saw nothing and we should turn back, but I stopped him and said, 'I will not rest until I find the poppies and save the queen.' Just then, I spotted a glimpse of red. . ." The knight continued, soaking in the attention.

Draven's carefree demeanor rapidly evaporated, and he froze in the crowd, listening as intently as the people around, but for a different reason.

The townsfolk collectively leaned in, anticipating the heroic ending where the brave knight picked the flower and raced home to save their queen. Draven strained to hear if that was his flower. The knight finally described the location and poppy with excitement, making Draven's heart sink to his belly.

Immediately, he backed out of the crowd, retrieved his waiting mule, and sprinted through the city gates at full speed. Taking a secret trail, Draven guided the mule easily, and soon they reached the spot where his precious poppies had always stayed hidden. A sliver of hope remained. *It has all been a mistake. It really hasn't been my own delicate flowers uprooted and pulverized to save some pathetic woman's life, has it?* As soon as they approached the secret spot, Draven jumped from the saddle, jarring his muscles and sending shots of pain through his weakening legs. "Argh!" he exclaimed in pain. "Why did that hurt so?" he asked the mule, sucking in breath through clinched teeth until the hurt receded. He inhaled deeply and shuffled forward, desperate to see what was no longer there. Hope evaporated. Branches lay rudely discarded, and where his beautiful bush once sat, a heap of upturned earth showed mockingly.

Panicked, Draven glanced at his hands, seeing the skin already loosening. His fingers ran through the short, thinning hair on top of his head, and he knew it was now streaked with silver. Even the simple act of reaching up tweaked his muscles, and he realized he ached from age. "I waited too long," he spoke to himself, distraught and angry. "Why did I wait too long? I thought I would have plenty of time, that's why. Now what?" A dark thought slid into his mind, clear as day. *They took everything from me. I will take it back.*

Mumbling, Draven devised a plan to retrieve his precious flower, knowing that it had been destroyed. "What if . . . what if the magic passed on to the queen? No, she's still bedridden in recovery. She obviously does not possess the powers of the poppy. The child! He was born healthy despite the long distress of the labor, and he flourishes. That must be it!" A wicked smile bloomed on his face. He was clearly pleased with his cleverness. Draven swung back onto his old mule with less ease than the day before. *I must hurry. The magic is wearing off too quickly.* Pulling the reins into the direction of the city, he kicked off, muscles tensed to do whatever it took.

✳ ✳ ✳

Night fell on the kingdom of Stillemäch, and the whole of the city was silent in their slumber. King and queen lay side by side in their large four-poster bed, deep sleep enrobing them in their exhausted state of new parenthood. Freshly changed and belly blissfully full, the sweet babe lay under the open window, dreaming of new faces, shapes, and colors. Warm air drifted in and out of the room, dancing around the chamber like spritely spirits of summer. All was well and all were unaware.

Small sounds of strain escaped the mouth of a lone figure as he hoisted the grapple high overhead. Cloaked in dark robes, Draven exhausted the last of the magic running through his veins, braced himself, and scaled the castle wall. Grapple scraped softly against stone, but held tight as he hoisted himself up the long rope, one foot at a time. Toes tapped along the cold wall, searching for a foothold just large enough to rest in. His muscles shook from the strain, his hands ached from the grip, but alas he climbed with vigor knowing he would soon be young and strong again.

Finally, the exhausted man reached the balcony of the royal chamber and hoisted himself over with immense effort. Landing on the stone floor with a heavy thud, he crouched low, still as a gargoyle, waiting for any sign of alarm. All he heard, however, was the wind whispering in his ears and the low sounds of deep sleep. Slowly, he straightened from his crouch and walked forward, grateful for the easy access to the chamber that the open window provided. *One less obstacle to deal with.* He slipped through the frame and, laying directly in front of him, surrounded by draped panels of chiffon, was the royal bassinet. Draven tiptoed to the baby's bedside and peeked in. The tiny infant lay still as he slept, peacefully unaware. The tiny chest raised up and down with every breath, and his miniature lips puckered, sucking automatically. Reaching down, he noticed once again how aged his skin looked even since this very afternoon, and he touched the baby's bald head. As quietly as possible, he chanted his incantation. Just as he suspected, the power surged from the baby and filled his limbs with the familiar strength.

Once restored to his youthful self, Draven swaddled the little body tightly and scooped the bundle up into his arms. Jostled awake, the tiny prince wailed instantly. Dreamily, Barrett rolled over, not easily woken, but Felicity immediately opened her eyes, as if she had been expecting something dreadful to happen. Her heart raced as she jumped from her bed, the feather duvet thrown to the side, and a chill flew through her body as her toes landed on the cold floor. But the cold was not what made her freeze. She stood suddenly helpless, the sensation of ice water coursing through her body as a dark figure clutching her baby tightly, tucked in the crook of his arm, jumped from the balcony of their chamber into the darkness below. The queen's screams were once again heard throughout the castle.

Soldiers, knights, squires, and peasants all tirelessly searched the entire night, and every day after for weeks, but the illusive dark figure was never found. Each day the seekers left with rekindled hope, returning home with nothing to deliver but heartache. Finally, with resources exhausted and still no trace of the evil man nor royal infant, there was nothing more to be done. Quietly standing on the balcony, willing the location of her child reveal itself, she heard Barrett step lightly behind her. "I know," she said softly without a word from her husband. Delicate hands rested on the balustrade, her slender chin held high and proud, but silent tears gave away her inner turmoil.

Barrett closed the gap between them, resting his hands on her shoulders, as if touching her might result in shattered pieces. When she leaned back into his chest, he slid his arms around in comfort. "It's time to call it off," he nearly whispered, planting a gentle kiss on her neck. Commanding and immovable in public, a tear on the side of his cheek brushed against Felicity's jaw, giving him away.

She turned around, finding comfort in his tall, strong frame as thick arms wrapped around a little tighter. "I know," she repeated, feeling his bearded chin lower onto the crown of her sandy head, "but that's my baby out there, and I will never forget him." With heavy hearts, they called off the search, and the king and queen were forced to move forward with their lives. However, every year on their first son's birthday, they honored his life with a volley of cannon fire, making sure that one cannonball was shot for every year without their sweet baby boy.

4

TOWER FOR ONE

SEVENTEEN YEARS LATER

Exploding in the sky, rays of the summer sun broke over the horizon in breathtaking beauty, as it did every morning. Before the first beam of light crossed over the darkness of the land, he was awake, watching from the steep stone window. Sitting still, he studied the way the sun slowly but consistently lit up the entire world, an inch at a time.

In all directions, as far as he could see, the world was covered in a forest that grew denser every year. This meadow was the only place where the thickness of the trees broke up for miles around, and being at such a high vantage point, he truly could see both near and far. Covered in a variety of wild grasses and colorful wildflowers, the meadow allowed a limited view of the world below before bushes and saplings began to pop up as a precursor to the trees. Varying trees, both large and small, thick and thin, leaves and needles. He'd studied every type of tree he could see using the Dutch invention called a telescope, comparing with species in his thick book on dendrology. He reviewed leaf patterns, growth requirements, uses, and so on to break up the daily routine.

When not studying about saplings and timber, the young man placed the textbook on a shelf next to astronomy, biology, mythology, and more. Literature of all kinds lined the shelves, keeping his mind occupied during the solitary days. Along with the sciences, adventure, and mysteries, historical tales of conquering and revenge all aided in giving him a tiny glimpse as to what life must be like beyond this lonely meadow and past the sea of trees.

On the shelf above the thick textbooks were sixteen works on the subject of soldiering, worn from overuse, including *Weaponry, Combat: Swordsmanship, Combat: Hand to Hand, Stories of Famous Battles,* and *Forging Your Own*. Read and re-read a hundred times, practiced and perfected, the art of battle spoke to him. His skills grew daily and knowledge continued to expand as he was aware of and harnessed the intensity inside. Inhaling deeply, he turned to his only friend, a young falcon raised from a hatchling. "Today is the day." He spoke solemnly, breaking the silence. Valk cocked her neck inquisitively, then bowed a feathered head, nudging his sleeve. "Yep, you're right," he responded, smiling at her persistence. "Can't do anything until breakfast." With that, Ransom swung his legs back inside, dropped to the stone floor, and headed to the main tower.

His chamber sat on the east end of the old ruins in what was once a great and mighty castle. Oftentimes he thought of the pirates that came from faraway lands to attack and raid as he walked the hall, passing giant arched windows. Not only did the advance turn into a ferocious battle crossing steel, but both sides had dragons as well. When the fight ended, the castle had been completely destroyed except this tower. Ruined, the palace was no longer desirable, as damage had been too devastating for both the blood-thirsty pirates and surviving royalties, resulting in both parties moving on. The tall stone tower became abandoned and eventually forgotten in history. When younger, Ransom would stop halfway down the hall and gaze across the meadow, imagining dragons and pirates spilling from the trees.

Curious as always, he scanned the meadow floor, but not for creatures of fairytales. Instead, he looked for deer and hares, foxes and polecats, any wildlife that might already be out and about, just as eager to catch a glimpse of the simple life as he had been about mythical life. Underneath his feet, two large fortified arches supported his path, allowing for critters to occasionally wander without determent when crossing the wide open glen.

Entering the main tower, Ransom crossed the floor to a table, opened the bread box sitting on top, and pulled out a round lump freshly baked the day before. The look was not quite to his liking yet, but the taste more than made up for its inadequate appearance. Setting the rough-looking loaf down, he cut two neat slices: one thin and one nice and thick. He put the rest back in the box and walked to the window facing north. He whistled, and the falcon zoomed into place, landing gracefully beside her friend, then pecked presumptuously at the bread that lay by her talons.

The main tower was larger than his own chamber, although small enough to feel stifling at times, and contained all the necessities to maintain a comfortable, solitary life. On one side of the room all the culinary essentials sat neatly organized. Cook stove, pots and pans, dishes, pump for water, table with two chairs, and the basics for household maintenance. A wash tub and trunk full of linens sat on the other end of the small room near the fireplace, along with another wall of overflowing bookshelves.

Ransom watched Valk peck at her food, then pulled out some jerky. "Huh, almost empty. Good thing Father comes today." He spoke to his companion on an equal level. As commanded, Ransom stayed safely in the tower, while father visited several times a week to provide resources, always keeping the tower well stocked. Along with food, he would bring larger clothing and boots, new subjects to read, writing supplies, targets and weapons for practice, and so on.

The young man became lost in the view out the large window, searching past the trees as he did more and more these days, yearning for adventure, longing for companionship, and searching for purpose. "I wish I could shoot my own game for once. I feel like I'd be a great hunter if I were given the chance. Or forage. Just to reach into the earth for mushrooms and tubers, feel the soft dirt for once. Even buying wares and meeting new faces. I hate sitting up here helpless." Ransom sighed and turned to his friend. "What's it like to have the freedom to come and go, Valk? Flying over the evil world. Do you see the misery?" The world was full of wickedness, he'd been told countless times, waiting to destroy him just as it had destroyed this once mighty castle.

From a very young age, Ransom often asked questions about the world below. "Father, why must I stay when you go?" he would ask with big blue eyes, so sad and lonely.

"My son, I would love you by my side, but I keep you here to protect you," Draven would always respond. "I've told you before what the world is like. Your life is not something I am willing to risk." He would then spend time telling stories of otherworldly wickedness and havoc. Witches and warlocks awaited to suck the souls from young, brazen men. Creatures of the night dragged unsuspecting victims into their dark caverns, never to be seen again. Sirens in the ocean lured men to their watery graves. Of course, these were all fairytales that Father would tell a curious boy, but as he grew older, Ransom started thinking and questioning.

As his mind developed and changed, stories changed as well, from things of make-believe to real-world evils. Every visit to his son, Draven reminded the young man of his differences, and how simple minds were afraid of different. "Fear drives people to do evil, and they would not hesitate to kill," he often said. Others would greedily capture Ransom for his power, using it for their gain. Captivity, torture, imprisonment, suffering. That was how the world worked. The frightening tales of the real outside worked just as Draven hoped, and Ransom obediently stayed in the protective confines of his tower, high above the world, without thought or longing. Alas, time passed, allowing the boy to mature and grow in stature. Then one day, a piece of paper changed everything.

Flipping through a used text entitled *Birds of Prey, Volume II* that he had received for his sixteenth birthday, Ransom noticed a corner of yellowed paper out of place. He grabbed the tiny edge and slid out a pamphlet. Elegant scroll announced with pride "Stillemäch Vanquishes Evil Once Again!" and Ransom's heart skipped a beat. Was it true? Were there people who actually fight for good? He continued reading:

> Ye royal cavalry of Stillemäch once again vanquishes evil. The invasion from the north of wild, uncivilized brutes, namely ferocious Vikings, pillaged and destroyed many farms across the border of our sister kingdom Noctura. Called upon to assist, our brave soldiers fought back the hoard of barbarians and won victory for the good.
>
> Hurrah for Stillemäch!

His eyes immediately lit up with astonishment. *Armies of valiant men that fought for good.*

"I can't believe it," he gasped. "Where is this place? How can this be? He said there was no good in the world." In an instant the world beyond was a different place, full of hope and possibilities. "Why did Father lie?"

The questions accumulated and tumbled in his mind. His heart pounded with equal parts excitement and anxiety, wanting to share the treasured pamphlet, but also afraid. After spending his entire life above an untouchable world, Ransom realized his father's one-sided portrayal was an incredible betrayal.

The thought made him sick. "How could he keep me up here like a sculpture made of glass? I'm far from breakable or corruptible. He had no faith in me or my abilities, even with my powers." Though he still loved was father, the hurt ran deep. "Why?" he asked himself. Frustration boiled inside. "Why would he keep this from me?" Ransom shouted to the empty space, trying to understand. Silence answered back, allowing room for reflection. In the stillness, Ransom felt something unexpected and realized relief ran deeper. Contrary to everything he had been taught, there really were good people fighting for justice and *vanquishing evil.* "No more hiding."

Living in fear was no longer an option, and he would never again allow it to rule his life. What was the point in possessing great strength if he never used it to protect others from the evils that haunted his own dreams? Something inside Ransom changed. Since that day, he silently committed to leave. Hours of loneliness transformed into the perfect opportunity to train in combat, master the art of weaponry, exercise, and harness his strength, while learning the specifics of war through thick books that now contained torn and wrinkled pages from overuse.

For two years, Ransom had been planning his heroic arrival into the world below, and for two years he had been working up the courage to ask his father's permission, as it was the only obstacle he faced. Draven had never given Ransom leave for even a minute. Dutifully and respectfully, the boy had obeyed his father's wishes, remaining above, watching every sunrise and sunset, completing daily chores and training in between. As each day passed, he renewed his hope that the morrow would bring the opportunity he'd been waiting for.

Clapping palms together to rid his hands of crumbs from the small meal, Ransom spoke to his friend, putting voice to his thoughts as if they had been in the middle of conversation. "I'm going to do it. How could he say no?" He posed the question to his feathered friend, who answered back by nipping for a little dried meat. "You're right, I'm almost eighteen. A man by any standards. Surely, he can't say no now." Valk responded by bobbing her feathery head up and down pleasantly, but a second later screeched a warning, high and sharp. The abrupt alarm would seem random to most, but Ransom understood perfectly. She screeched once more, announcing the arrival of a visitor.

"Ransom! Ransom! Pull me up," a deep voice bellowed from far below. Waiting impatiently, Draven looked up from under the tower's window, surrounded by a collection of sacks. The thick gray back of the old mule ambled close by, already contentedly grazing. Ransom gave a hearty wave, then turned quickly to slip on the inconvenient gloves he was supposed to constantly wear. The thin leather forming perfectly to his large hands protected the skin from injury that could result in complete loss of powers, but to a seventeen-year-old it felt overly cautious. With palms protected, he grabbed a secret vine laying among the ordinary, then pulled back easily. A small area surrounding Draven began to rise as a square platform, camouflaged among the grasses, emerged from the greenery below.

Ransom lifted the load with no note of strain, sweat never breaking across his brow, as his father and the load of supplies ascended to the window's ledge. As soon as the platform was raised to full height, the young man wrapped the vine around a strong pole inside the room, securing the lift and freeing his hands. With light feet, he crossed the area quickly, eager to help unload supplies.

"It took you long enough, son. You're slacking. Are you forgetting to work your muscles daily?" Draven asked dryly with his chin purposefully raised to look down on the young man. This act did very little since the boy was now several inches taller than his father and still growing. Draven untied his black cloak, hung it on a hook by the window, and loosened his sleeves.

"No, sir. I'm exercising, studying, and cleaning every day, just as you have instructed," Ransom replied, unloading the commodities while his father rested at the table. "Sorry for the delay. It won't happen again."

Draven waited to reply, letting the apology linger in the air for a moment, then finally relaxed slightly, swiping a hand over his short silver beard. The look on his face tightened, morphing from annoyance to stern rebuke. "Don't ever apologize. It shows weakness. Just do better next time. Always be better." Then the weariness of his trip settled over his shoulders like a thick wet blanket. "Speaking of weak. Come close, son. Allow this old man to feel young again."

"Of course, Father." The young man stepped forward, standing in front of the man in black. Draven placed wrinkled hands on the broad shoulders of the youth, and Ransom closed his eyes, concentrating on the words as always. "Strengthen marrow, strengthen bones. Time reversed, stand all alone. Recover, revive, redeem, renew. Become the person that I once knew." Power surged, the younger feeling it leaving his body as the elder felt it flooding his own.

When Ransom opened his eyes, the man standing before him was once again youthful and handsome. Draven smiled and clapped his hands on the young, strong shoulders with delight. "Well done, my boy. Now, would you like to see what I've brought for you? I shot a buck not too far from here and packed out the meat. We'll need to get it drying before nightfall. Honey from the bees in the clover field. More staples: flour, salt, that sort of thing." He pulled several linen sacks from a larger bag, all tied securely with string. "A new book. I thought you might enjoy ornithology this time."

Ransom nodded without hearing most of the words, "Father, I have a ques—"

Draven interrupted. "Some new arrows. I know you broke most of yours during the last couple weeks so I bought more. They were a bit pricey, but I guess I'm just a really great father."

Ransom accepted the arrows. "That's wonderful. I'm so grateful for all of this, but could you slow down for a minute? I have a ques—"

"And new clothing! We can't have you turning eighteen with high trousers and a shirt that's bursting at the seams, now could we? A new leather vest to top it off. Oh, I know the blue was a little over the top. Should've gone with brown, but this was a good deal—uh, I mean I just knew it would look good on you."

"Father. Just stop!" Ransom finally burst with frustration.

The man halted his riflings through bags of newly acquired goods and looked up, confused. "Did I purchase the wrong arrows again?"

"No. The arrows are fine." He lay the new, small arsenal on the table. "Father, I just . . . I mean . . . "

"Well, spit it out, man! Don't whimper and stammer. Stand up straight and speak like a man." Draven rolled his shoulders back, puffing out his own chest in demonstration.

Ransom took one final breath, straightened up instantly, and peered straight into his father's dark eyes. "I'm ready. I'm ready to leave this tower, and I'd like your permission to do so." He spoke with an even tone, clutching his fists to stop the nervous shaking.

Whatever Draven was expecting, this was not it, and a moment passed as he gathered his thoughts. "What are you ready for, exactly?" Draven finally asked, instantly icy. "Are you ready to be hunted down? Or locked away like a pet so someone can use your power whenever they please? Are you ready for manipulation? Not to mention ruination, castration, ostentation, strangulation. The world is full of darkness, my son—"

"Exactly," Ransom cut his father off. "Darkness, pain, grief. Some things you can't prevent, but some things you can. Father, there are terrible people in this world. You have taught me that all my life. It's taken me eighteen years to figure out my calling, what I'm meant to be, but now I understand why I'm different. I have strength beyond any measure and power to heal. What kind of man would I be if I stayed here my whole life, cowering from who or what might be? There is evil out there—you've told me horrible stories—and I may well be the only one who can actually do something about it." He straightened his shoulders and stood even taller. "I'm ready to become a knight and join the Royal Cavalry. I could fight for justice and freedom, vanquish the spiteful, and heal good people in the process."

Draven's blood ran cold at the thought of his prized possession leaving forever.

"This is my destiny, Father. Can't you see that? Would you give me permission?"

Rage boiled up from deep within Draven's core, and he turned his back to Ransom until he gained control over his facial expressions. Regaining composure, he faced the boy again with an overly cheerful smile on his thin lips that did not match the darkness in his eyes. "What a noble, ambitious heart you have. I'm so proud of you, son."

Ransom's eyes brightened with hope. "Really? You are? Oh, thank you, Father! So I have your permission to go?"

"Well, no. Ransom, I have listened to all you have to say, but I don't take any of it lightly. We must make sure you're properly trained, that you're well read, and that you know how to care for yourself before you go off on your own."

"But, Father," Ransom pleaded, brushing a stray lock of sandy hair from his face, smoothing it back in place among the others. "I *have* been preparing . . . "

"Ransom. That is enough. You are not ready yet, but if this is what you truly want, we will get you ready. Have some patience, my boy. Nothing great happens instantly." Draven stepped forward, swinging his black cloak on and tying it back in place. "I must be off. Re-read your armory literature, and continue with target practice. When you're ready, truly ready, we'll talk about it again. Until then, I don't want to hear another word about leaving. I must go check my traps now, but I will be back tomorrow. Take care of that venison." With finality, the older man walked onto the suspended platform and nodded at the boy.

Draven's words were comforting on the surface, but the meaning was dark. *You will never be ready, and the world will never know of your existence. If I have to bind you for eternity and burn every vine reaching this window, I will do so with a jubilant heart. I will never let you out of here.*

Ransom unwound the thick vine dutifully, slowly lowering his father down to the ground far below. As the platform landed back on solid ground, he tied the vine on the ledge, securing it in place, and stumbled back to the table. Rifling through the sacks of provisions, all he felt was the deep disappointment of failure. He failed to convince his father, failed to secure approval, failed the people he could have helped. With a heavy heart, Ransom left the new supplies where they sat in disarray and wandered back down the hall to his own chamber. Pulling an old, well-read book off a shelf, he began to console his bruised spirit with tales of knights on the battlefield.

When I'm ready. It'll happen when I'm ready.

5

RUNAWAY

Faster. The quick strike of a small, springy branch slapped her across the forehead. Although it hurt, the thin bough did nothing to slow her down, but the thick root sticking up did. One of her ill-fitting boots hit a solid arch bowing from the ground. The tree itself stood firm, mocking as she fell hard. Her hands sprung out quickly, slowing the bulk of the downward force before her face met ground. But even with quick reflexes, the rest of her body fell with a jarring thud. Gasping like a fish out of water, trying to blink away the dancing pin-pricks of light, she allowed herself to lay still for only a moment.

Once she regained her breath and sight, she strained to listen over the thud of her heart. Nothing. The forest was soundless in an alive sort of way. Leaves gently rustled above her head. *Wait, what was that?* Her heart picked up the pace as she heard a slow shuffling through the trees. Could it be a bear or boar? Then a familiar *ting ting* jingled ever so softly through the air like a tiny wood sprite dancing through the trees. The musical sound terrified the lost girl, and her heart now sprinted in place. Many of the guards didn't care to waste time fastening the small brass buckles on the sides of their boots, and the little metal pieces on each leg moved with the rhythm of the man. When he stepped hard or quick, the little *ting* sound was audible enough.

Out of her element, she had no way of judging distance, but he didn't sound too far away. *Keep moving,* she told herself. Slowly, her head lifted as she backed up, carefully looking around. With no one in sight, she pushed up to a crouch, legs shifting for support. The boots on her feet gave an identical *ting ting* sound, as if answering the sprite's call, and her heart froze in the same instant as her body. *How could I forget that these boots make the same noise?* She waited, willing her heart to beat again. *Did he notice?*

Holding her breath, she listened for a moment longer, but the sound of the soldier's buckle seemed to be fading. Without waiting for confirmation, she pushed off the leafy ground and darted in the opposite direction like a rabbit scared out of hiding. Looking over her shoulder, she ran smack into something thick and solid. Quickly, muscled arms wrapped around her body, turning her roughly for a better hold. "Thought you could run?" he sneered, pinning her back against his chest. Stale, acrid breath invaded her senses as she struggled to breathe. "A pretty little princess wouldn't last a night alone in this forest!"

"Good thing I'm not a princess," she barely choked out, jabbing her elbow hard into the man's thick gut. Stunned by the unexpected sharp jab, the brute doubled over just as she rotated her arm upward, the small but solid fist meeting square in the bridge of his nose. Immediately, his grip on the girl released, and she ripped herself out of his arms, bolting forward without a glance back. Angry howls from an injured man echoed from behind, luckily becoming softer with distance.

Don't look back. Keep running. They'll never give up. Even with oversized, worn-out boots, she moved with the grace of a frightened doe, sleek and graceful, weaving through the trees. Fear propelled her forward, and adrenaline kept her going. *Just keep running,* she thought as she covered more ground, grateful for the early hour. *It's barely morn. Plenty of time to find a place to hide.*

Her big brown eyes constantly darted from side to side, searching for sanctuary. Her black hair was semi-contained, tied low at the neck, and she flipped the big gray hood overhead. The wide capuche draped loosely, but completely. Even without a mirror, she knew this disguise made her look like a man, or more specifically a guard from the kingdom of the south, Lôunarike. *No one will try bothering me now.*

Her boots continued to shuffle through the sparse greenery of the forest floor, slowing with each hour. Knowing she had most likely evaded the guards by now, she listened for wilder predators. The idea of four-legged furry beasts picking up her scent frightened her nearly as much as the idea of being captured again, and she began speaking her thoughts aloud to possibly thwart any ideas a bear or lion might have about lunch.

"Didn't I pass these trees already? No, I'm pretty sure I've kept north, or was that northeast? Either way, I've been consistent, I think. Blast these branches, blocking the sun like they own it!" Frustratingly, every animal den or creek bend seemed a duplicate of the last as well, disorienting the girl more and more. "Am I going in circles?" she mumbled, taking comfort from the sound of her own voice. Aimlessly, she continued to wander.

A deep growl let her know she had gone without one too many meals, and she lay her hand on her midsection to stifle the cry. Soon she would rest, and that would be the time to forage for whatever the forest had to offer. As she pushed on and stumbled farther, the trees faded away, leaving a wide open meadow. The unexpected opening gave welcome relief from the overbearing forest, and she tried to remain in control. Slowly, she scanned the area to be sure she was alone, like a hesitant doe entering open grazing grounds. On the far side of the glen, a pile of ruins prevailed from what appeared to once have been a castle. All that remained was a lonely tower, standing high and solitary.

The fallen fortress, as well as the entire clearing, looked completely deserted. No cave or hollow log was large enough, and she needed shelter fast to hide and rest. Safety, freedom, and life depended on whether or not she could find a place out of sight. Looking around one more time, she sighed, knowing the only option stood across the meadow, appearing high enough to touch the clouds.

Braving the open, she crossed the grassy field, timidly at first, but with more confidence when no alarm was heard. Fears melted as fascination took over. Stones scattered before her, telling of a time long ago. Large pieces lay strewn in various heaps, and a few enormous boulders sat off by themselves looking humble and lonely. As she approached the only standing section of the once mighty fortress, she noted that vines climbed up the rough wall on the west end and not the other. "I guess this is the side I'll climb," she mumbled, peering toward the sky. Her hands brushed against the thick vines, rustling hearty leaves gently as she picked the thickest one. It looked sturdy enough and appeared to reach all the way to the window's ledge above. Leaning back, she tested the strength of the vine. It held firm. "Well, here goes nothing." Confidence waning, she hoisted her body up, gripping tight. One foot settled against the vertical stone, then the other. As she pulled her body higher, she braced the weight against the wall with large, flimsy boots.

Brick by brick, one hand over the other, she made her way deliberately up the tower. Twice, the ill-fitting footwear slipped, but arms flexed and hands tightened just in time to delay falling long enough for her feet to reposition themselves. The uniform was heavy on her slight frame, the immense effort and strain forcing her tired body to break out in sweat. Droplets formed around her hairline, sliding slowly in trails around the edge of her jaw. Muscles started to shake and hands began to weaken. *I can do this.* Incredibly, her hands gripped firmly long enough to reach the ledge. Fingertips brushed over the coarse edge of the thick opening, and the thought of being so close propelled her up and over. Finally, she stood on a solid, clean floor.

As her pupils adjusted to the dimmer light, she became completely stunned. Lining the walls were amenities she had not expected to see: a clean cook stove, pots and utensils without a speck of dust, a simple mirror, dishes freshly washed. On the other end of the room was a fireplace, clean but frequently used, and other objects such as a wash basin and large kettle suggested that the place wasn't as abandoned as she expected. A table sat in the center of the room, clean and polished, with a pair of matching chairs. On top lay a pile of provisions, newly acquired from the looks of it. She stepped forward, pulled in by curiosity, and began examining the wares. Linen sacks of flour and salt, clothing, fresh meat. This tower not only had had visitors, but it clearly had a resident that had been here this morning. For the first time she wondered if the person was actually still here right now. Prickles crawled up the back of her neck at the thought, and she began to scour the room once more, this time for any signs of life. Turning, she sensed a presence. Her heart leapt into her throat from fear and surprise a second before all the world went dark.

6

INTRUDER

Snapping the book shut, Ransom brooded over the injustice that was his life. *Why? Why won't he let me go? It's not fair. I feel like a prisoner. Father is just overly protective.* "How can I finally prove myself?" he posed the question to the empty room before hanging his head low in defeat. *When will it be enough?*

Thoughts swirled like a constant tornado, destructive and confusing. He dropped the book, and, with his elbows on knees, rested hands on the back of his head. Sitting still, he tried to calm all thoughts and clear his mind, but a rustling sound interrupted the stillness, and he wondered which small creature was flittering on the vines today. Occasionally, squirrels or birds explored the leafy creepers on the west tower, and Ransom pictured the critters scampering or fluttering in and out of the ivy. A smile broke across stoic lips. In such a solitary life, animals that frequented the air around his tower and the meadow below were the only friends he had ever known.

Valk, the closest of his friends, appeared, landing on Ransom's windowsill, and screeched in alarm. He snapped to attention. "Are you sure, Valk? He can't be back already. He said not 'til tomorrow." The bird sounded off again, and Ransom pushed himself up. Crossing the room, he reached the sill and peered down, seeing nothing out of the ordinary. The rustling sounded closer. He swept his eyes over the vine just in time to spy a man struggling to pull himself up. Blood drained from his face as the uninvited guest finally made it over the window's ledge on the other end of the tower.

Panic took over, and he backed away from the open window, search-ing for a place to hide. *They've finally come for me, just as Father said. They're here to capture me. I'll be a prisoner the rest of my life!* Initial panic faded to resolve as his eyes fell over the collection of weapons in the corner and zeroed in on a small club. He knew he must fight.

Ransom lifted the short, well-formed weapon from the floor and qui-etly stepped out of his room. Light footed, he made his way down the hall, listening for movement. The sounds coming from the west end were quiet and delayed. The intruder inside his home shuffled slowly, not with the brisk determination he would expect from a man bent on attack. When he reached the end of the hall, Ransom peeked through the open door-way into the room beyond. The stranger stood with his back to the hall, studying the new provisions. *So, he's here to loot first, then take me captive.* The man seemed short, but size meant very little when it came to combat. Ransom knew a smaller man could easily out-maneuver a larger opponent with agility and training.

The uninvited guest surveyed the contents on the table, leaving the provisions where they lay for now. *He'll never have the opportunity to take anything from this place.* Moving closer without making a sound, Ransom was almost within swinging distance when the cloaked figure suddenly looked up, as if sensing the presence of another. The hood began to turn, deliberately scanning the room, and Ransom was afraid that the sound of his heartbeat would give away his position long before the enemy lay eyes on him. In one second he'd lose his advantage. That could not happen.

The covered face turned at the same time that Ransom's arm swung up and quick as lightning struck down. He swung with enough force to knock the stranger down, but was careful enough that there shouldn't be any real damage. The small club made contact with the back of the skull, and the thumping sound was dulled by the thick wool of the hood. Immediately, the stranger went limp and fell to the floor. Standing over the unconscious body, Ransom released the breath he had been holding. *Now, what to do with this villain? Throw him over the edge of the tower? No, that's too cold-hearted. Wake him up and force him to climb back down? Seems unlikely and will probably result in the fight that I'm trying to avoid. Tie him up and ask questions? That might be the best way to know what I'm dealing with, if he tells the truth.*

Ransom squatted down, observing the stranger's clothing. He was a guard, most likely. The crest on the upper left of the chest meant he must be from Lôunarike. *The History of Famous Battles* in his collection contained illustrations of many crests from all the great kingdoms, and Ransom had read that same thick book six times. He looked at the hood. Why was he covered up on this sunny day? The only answer Ransom could come up with was to be unnoticed. But why? To hide, or to be hidden? Either way, it was suspicious.

The chest of the unconscious man, thickly padded for protection, rose and fell with shallow breaths. Ransom nudged the side of the ribs, but still the only movement came from the lungs. Satisfied the guard was out cold, he knocked back the hood quickly.

Ransom stumbled back, suddenly caught off guard with the new revelation. Long black lashes rested lightly above prominent cheekbones as eyes remained shut. The nose sloped down smoothly, and lips were incredibly full; nothing like he had ever seen in real life. The skin was darker than his, flawless too, and those cheeks had a slight flush of red from heat, no doubt created by the heavy thickness of the uniform. Lying still on the stone floor, shallow breath came slowly in and out of her barely parted lips. Black strands of hair fell over her face randomly, curling at the roots from the moisture of sweat and heat, but the majority of the thick mane was pulled back low.

Awkwardly, Ransom searched her pockets for weapons, correspondence, or random objects that might help to identify this woman. Patting along her hips, his hand landed on something bulky and hard. Slowly, he reached into the pocket and pulled out a necklace. Gold glistened as the thick chain stretched out in front of his face, hanging long and heavy in his hand. Even though the links were simple, the superb quality was obvious, punctuated by the pendant hanging on the end. A large rectangular emerald, almost the size of his palm, was surrounded in delicate golden filigree. The jewel suspended from the chain, appearing weightless, though quite the hefty treasure.

Ransom studied the unconscious woman, then the jewelry in his hand. His brows furrowed.

Was she sent as a spy to find and capture me? Is this her payment? Why a woman?

Pocketing the trinket for now, he crossed the room to an old chest containing Draven's knick-knacks and fished out a rope. Sliding her body across the floor, he wrapped the rope around slender wrists and legs, then propped her against the wall. *Now what?*

With nervous energy, he began tidying the room, putting the linen sacks away, straightening furniture, and washing items that were already clean. The work did little to calm his nerves, and he found himself taking a seat next to the bound girl, boot tapping with anticipation. *A woman. What do I say when she wakes up? How do I act?* He'd read about women in books, both fiction and nonfiction, and imagined how they spoke softly and glided gracefully, but so far everything imagined had been completely wrong. Nowhere in the stories had there been a female guard, a woman strong enough to climb a tower, or a lady killer.

Eyes began to flutter slowly as she drifted into consciousness, mists of confusion evaporating slowly from the depths of her mind. Memories swirled, images coming back little by little. *Leaving, running, climbing. A strange tower.* Brown eyes burst open, an act she immediately regretted. Sharp pain shot through the back of her head with the sudden blast of light. Lids defensively clamped shut, her face going askew as a bolt of pain struck again quickly, a headache reverberating in her skull. Raising her hands to cradle her wounded head, her wrists moved in tandem, tied together. *What is going on?* A second later, she realized her ankles were unable to move as well.

The fog finally cleared from her muddled brain, and her eyes peeked open, cautiously this time. Determined to spy the villain, she braced herself, pushing through the pain, and was surprised by the sight of a young man sitting in a chair, eagerly staring back. He leaned forward, resting on his forearms, blue eyes looking both curious and apprehensive as they studied her every move. Neither spoke for a moment. Then he broke the tension by sweeping back a piece of sandy blond hair, barely long enough to tuck behind his ear.

He's tall, she discerned. *Broad shoulders and large boots. What's with the gloves?*

His hands rested forward, fingers interwoven as he studied back with equal measurement, patiently waiting for her rattled brain to steady.

With a clear head, she choked down panic, fully grasping her position as captive to this stranger, and attempted to jerk her arms apart. *It's no use.* Trying again, she twisted harder, attempting to loosen the knot.

"Don't bother," he said, looking concerned and a tiny bit smug. "I'm excellent with knots, and I promise I tied this one so it won't come loose."

The comment, boastful but lighthearted, stopped her for a moment, and she looked up from her feeble attempt at escape. Summoning courage, she decided to speak, hoping this man would respond to a strong woman of authority. "Where am I?" she demanded, trying to sound dignified instead of terrified. "Who are you?"

"I think I'll do the questioning for now, if you don't mind, since I seem to be the one with the upper hand," he said firmly, matching her authority as his heart beat with excitement. Keeping his hands clasped to stop them from shaking nervously, he tried to appear in control, though inside he was a wreck of confusion. "Now, let's start with the obvious. Who sent you, and why are you here? Were you sent to capture me?" Ransom asked, leaning forward to better study her reactions.

"What?" she burst out, clearly surprised. "You captured me!" Her arms lifted in unison to remind the man of her current status.

A bird of prey landed on the windowsill and gave a small, piercing screech in her direction, startling the newcomer. Strangely, Ransom stood, crossed the room, and stroked his finger lightly on the feathers of the falcon's breast. "There, there, Valk. Be still. She is no threat." He then spoke to the maiden on the floor, all the while facing his friend. "Don't act so innocent. I know you're not here for the view. You came to find someone. To find me! Now who sent you?" While his back was turned, she reached forward into the shaft of her boot and pulled a small dagger from its narrow leather sheath. Flipping the blade quickly, aiming the sharp point toward herself, she began sawing on the rope. Turning, he saw her futile efforts and shrugged. "I wouldn't bother with that if I were you."

"Oh yeah," she said through gritted teeth, working quickly, "and why not?"

Ransom crossed his arms again, a slight smile playing on his lips, now amused with his prisoner. *She is determined, I'll gave her that. Probably will try sawing that cord the rest of the day if I don't stop her.* "I wouldn't bother because it is an enchanted rope. Nothing can cut through it. Not even your pretty little dagger." Reaching over, he nonchalantly plucked the small weapon from her awkward grip.

"How dare you! Gave that back!" she shouted, upset at the indignity of the entire situation. "Ugh. Fine." With no more tricks up her sleeve or down her boots, she relaxed slightly and leaned back against the wall again. "Please release me. I promise I am no threat to you."

"I'll be the one to determine that," he said lightly, twirling the small jeweled weapon in his hands. "Let's try this again. Who are you?"

Defiance flashed on her face, an automatic reaction of her fiery, spirited personality, but she folded quickly, releasing a sigh. "My name is Imelda," she stated simply, clearly uncomfortable revealing this small bit of information about herself.

"I'm going to need more than that, Imelda," he coaxed, smiling slightly.

Swallowing her pride, she began again. "My name is Imelda Vareal, lady to the Queen of the Emerald Coast, but I prefer to be called Mel." She looked at her captor, seeing interest but not eagerness, and somehow felt encouraged to continue. "I have no idea where I am, and I have no interest in you or in taking anyone captive."

Ransom listened, piecing the fragments of the puzzle together. When she paused, he jumped in. "Emerald Coast? But that's the kingdom of Smarahav. What are you doing with the crest of Lóunarike on your chest?" he asked, immediately flushing a soft pink. Pausing, a slight smile of embarrassment bloomed on his face, and the light of amusement gleamed in his eye. *Interrogator isn't really a position that suits me.*

Mel smiled back, momentarily entertained by his blunder and the slight discomfort he obviously felt. The embarrassment on his face and the way he lost his tough façade showed her that he was just as uncomfortable with the situation as she was. "Could I at least sit in a chair? It's kind of a long story."

7

EMERALD GATES

Daffodil-colored sand shifted as the ocean rolled in and out of tide. The combination of rich, flowing blue over warm yellow granules created an emerald effect across the shallows. Emerald Coast, one of the most spectacular destinations of the entire continent, was known, above all, for embodying beauty. Dignitaries, wealthy travelers, and even lowly wanderers were constantly drawn in by the promise of gorgeous beaches, magnificent views of divine coastal mountain ranges, the most intriguing art, exquisite food, and incredibly beautiful women.

Beauty. It was the largest commodity the kingdom of Smarahav offered. No natural ore or lead, gold, silver or brass. No copper underneath the towering mountains to mine and sell. Soil was not only deficient of any metal, but it also lacked even the basic chemical makeup to support hearty growth. The absence of nutrients in the land made the entire area inadequate for farming and the terrain unfit for most large grazing animals.

Even with scant natural resources, the kingdom thrived, flowing with commerce at the daily market, none of which were local. Vendors that sold wares in this city were travelers who brought items to peddle and stayed just long enough to spend most, if not all, of their earnings on pleasure. Booths contained a variety of spices, textiles, exotic fruits, and more, but the market also had basic wool, vegetables, grains, oils, wax and wicks, animals, and all other necessary products for everyday life. The only commodity produced in the city was art.

Sculptures, paintings, fashion, jewelry. If you were not beautiful by the king's standard, then the next best thing was to create beauty. A citizen lacking either talent was considered a leech, shunned from society and ulti-mately thrown out to dwell in the forest. Many failed to understand that the most beautiful city was also the ugliest underneath.

Imelda had lived in the castle on the coast all her life, training to be one of the Queen's Jewels. Imelda's parents, Count Fernando Vareal and Contessa Natalia, took pride in their only daughter's extraordinary beauty, for she was their rare diamond with thick ebony hair, full coral lips, and long lashes surrounding deep chocolate-brown eyes. Knowing they were blessed to have such a striking beauty, they took every advan-tage offered. When she was a toddler, the royal family took notice of the radiance in the child as well, a rare, natural exquisiteness they valued above all. Summoning the count and contessa to court, all agreed that the little lady would be raised to serve the queen, and in exchange her parents would receive luxuries, comfort, and favors.

The little Lady Imelda was brought up in a life of privilege and luxury, never wanting for anything. However, she paid dearly without a choice, and the price had been her free will. As a queen's Jewel, a young woman could do whatever she liked, as long as the queen approved. She was allowed to eat whatever she wanted, as long as the Queen recommended it. She was able to dress however she felt, so long as the dress was one the queen chose. She could marry whomever she desired, as long as her choice was picked from a short list of potential suitors vetted first by her royal majesty. The elegant balls, silks and furs, jewelry, rich foods, and extrav-agant accommodations had been appropriate compensation for the price of free will, of freedom, for most of the ladies, but it was never enough for Imelda. On the outside she was an obedient, high-born lady, but on the inside she longed to live free and choose her own path in life. Alas, there was no other life, so obediently and lavishly she lived.

Then the Great Drought descended on the land. Entire fields with-ered away, and weak stocks of barley and wheat turned golden and brit-tle before adequate seeds had the opportunity to grow. Hundreds of livestock died from hunger and thirst. Every kingdom, no matter how fortified, had been greatly affected, suffering countless losses. Smara-hav, however, was hit the hardest with ruin, the economy plummeting since wealth and basic supplies for the city relied almost entirely on out-side resources alone.. As the drought continued, travelers, peddlers, and merchants all desperately discontinued their travels, trying to salvage their own living matters. The Great Drought happened when Imelda had just turned fourteen years of age, and she witnessed the slow decline of luxuries, then of necessities.

Almost four years later, with the kingdom in immediate distress, the king and queen's royal advisers begged several kingdoms for financial assistance but were heartily refused. Finally, they received word back that the southern kingdom of Lôunarike had managed well enough to consider assisting the failing Smarahav, but not for free. Lôurian dignitaries had taken a special interest in the only truly valuable commodity Smarahav had to offer: beautiful women. Meeting with the king's royal council, the foreigners offered a proposal to help the kingdom recover financially until travel became fluent and the country was once again prosperous. The sum required for this kind of help was colossal, and the price that the declining province was required to pay was the seven most beautiful Smarahavie women.

Beauties were chosen quickly, as the most pleasing of the ladies were already kept in the castle, living to serve the queen. Imelda was among the seven and became a sacrifice without consent, so her people could regain their avaricious lifestyle. The king of Lôunarike did not send royal officials when it was time to collect their agreed upon payment, since the transportation of goods was considered menial work. Instead, he sent a company of twelve soldiers to secure and retrieve the cargo.

Though thousands of ramblers flowed in and out of the Emerald City every year, like the ocean flowing in and out on the yellow shores, this would be the first time any of these young ladies had ever exited the city gates. Bidding their families a proud, reluctant good-bye, the lovelies hesitantly climbed, one by one, into two dark carriages. Imelda, being the last to climb in, looked around but could not find the faces of her parents. Her heart broke as she realized they had already let her go, choosing to move on with the lavishness that the life of their only daughter had purchased. With tears threatening her vision, Imelda climbed into the carriage, appearing proud but feeling terrified.

Besides the ladies, a trunk had been secured on the back of the first carriage, collected from another realm when the guards had made their way to the Emerald Coast. The contents remained a mystery to all in the party, including the men who protected it. Curious as they were, they remained unknowing, as per their instructions. Perhaps knowing would have brought a little excitement to the trip, but as it were, each guard felt this trip was beneath their skill level. Not normally delivery men, the hardened soldiers considered the assigned escort of one trunk and several young women across the land to be tortuously mundane, and they begrudgingly carried out their orders without charm. Answers were kept short, if given at all. The days were long with minimal stops, and the ladies were treated with less kindness than a man gives his kine.

Settled snuggly in the cabs, the ladies were informed that the trip to the southern kingdom would take four to five days, depending on weather. Two days of hard travel took the party through the kingdom of Stillemäch, where they stopped for a short time to gather provisions, then continued out of the city and into the forest beyond. Even on a highway worn from frequent travel, the party's progress was slow. For a third night, the group of guards and maidens stopped, and the ladies were ordered to sleep upon the hard earth. Less than adequate, the food, accommodations, and courtesy offered to the young beauties created a feeling of tension as they all became more and more wary of their unknown future.

Regarded as completely harmless, as well as utterly useless, the ladies sat unguarded in the thick darkness of the forest while the guards settled in by the fire, drinking and laughing loudly. In the early night, perfumed heads bowed as the girls huddled together, miserable in every way. With every sniffle and shiver, the feeling of sovereign loyalty dissipated into the darkness, confusion left in its stead. Imelda looked around at the beautiful, forlorn faces, so close together they shared the same breath. As she commiserated with her sisters, a spark struck inside. Never once before that moment had she questioned her purpose in this world or her loyalty. She was born into a life she never picked, and always did her best to serve and obey, but being traded as a commodity was not a part of the deal.

Surrounded by girls ranging from as young as fifteen to eighteen needing direction, Imelda's spark ignited a fire. "Enough is enough," she finally spoke up, quiet but forceful. "Is this what we have been reduced to? It's unacceptable!" A low murmur began to churn among the group, as soft cries of vindication escaped the beautiful lips. In no time at all, Mel learned that the girls were not only lost and confused, but they were angry as well.

"How could our own people betray us so cruelly?" a girl spoke with a wavering voice.

"How has our queen let us go so easily?" another asked evenly. "I devoted my life to her!"

Another sitting across piped up, "We all did!"

"What were we even worth?" the youngest, just barely fifteen, squeaked.

Yes, all these ladies grew up on the Emerald Coast knowing what was valued in their land and what wasn't. They had strived for beauty and served their kingdom with unquestionable loyalty, but none ever expected to be reduced to a number and sold.

The more they whispered among themselves, the more bitterness crept in. Tears of sorrow dried up, determination replaced depression, and a new sense of self-worth crept into their small camp. Together, in the chilly air of the dark night, seven girls decided to take back their lives. They would leave the rude guards loudly snoring on the ground and together return to Smarahav to beg their beloved queen to take them back.

"That will never work," a feisty brunette insisted, obviously jaded.

Others still carried hope. "Surely she would see the folly in the kingdom's plan and seek another way to restore its greatness."

"Surely she misses us," the youngest added with hope.

Mel studied every face, listened to every word. "We have no money. Nothing to our names. I'm afraid we have no other choice."

"If we tell our queen how mistreated we have been since leaving the emerald gates, she will be furious. She has to be."

A soft-spoken girl spoke up. "Like a mother bear protecting her cubs. I read about that once." Silence fell over the group as they all realized that not even their own mothers had protected them.

Imelda nodded decisively. "It's settled. Just before dawn we'll run." Solemnly, they all agreed.

In the early hours of dawn, before the sun stretched the tips of its rays over the horizon's edge, the girls quietly sprung into action. Their dresses were too cumbersome, but luckily three nights camping in the rough showed the ladies that these guards preferred to shed their outer gear, only sleeping in their lighter underclothing. Strategically, each girl had picked a man and, in the early darkness, crept on bare feet to their side. Shaking from nerves, they snuck the thick outerwear away and dressed quickly. Moving with the grace of a lady, they disguised themselves in the form of men, swapping slippers for thick boots.

Six of the beauties had quickly donned the unflattering and foul-smelling uniforms, feeling bulky but freer to move around. The seventh, one of the younger girls, struggled into the thick top of the uniform. Nervously waiting, Imelda crept to the rear of the front carriage to check out the trunk on the back. Protected by two guards during the days, the treasure box sat unsupervised. As quietly as possible, she pulled the latch, finding it locked. Tugging again, she knew it was no use. The box would not open without its key. Then an idea sparked, and she reached into her large boot, where she had slipped her tiny dagger for safe keeping. Stealthily, she removed the fine, sharp blade and placed the tip into the little keyhole. It fit perfectly, only taking a second until the small mechanism clicked.

Her heart skipped a beat as she felt the cogs adjust. Looking around nervously, she lifted the lid just as a heavy thud banged loudly, disturbing the sleepy twilight. Her heart nearly leapt from her chest in surprise. Then tiny distinct jingling followed, ringing from the side of several pairs of scurrying boots. The struggling sister had tripped and fallen in her desperate attempt to finish dressing, and the others instinctively rushed to her aide before remembering the undone buckles. In the next instance, all erupted into mass chaos. Imelda reached into the box blindly, grabbed the first object her fingers touched, and tucked it quickly into her pocket. Seeing there was no way to reorganize the girls again, Imelda bolted in fright behind the carriages, praying her sisters would make it. She ran as fast as her weighed-down feet could move, never looking back. Running hard, she dodged trees and two soldiers for hours. For the first time in her life, she had chosen her own path, which led to a tall, dilapidated old tower.

8

SUN AND MOON

"Look at all those beautiful ladies," the princess sighed, gazing through the open frame of her chamber window high above the city streets. The cobblestones far below hummed with enterprise, lively and focused, as patrons and vendors carried about their various errands from near and far. "I love this time of year. It's like magic is in the air." Bobbing around happily, big, blue eyes circled back to her lady-in-waiting, seeking more from the stiff caretaker than the usual *hmph* she normally offered. Instead, the woman sat silent, making the soft *zwhir* sound of thread drawing through tightly woven material the only response as she continued pulling needle and thread in and out of a taut cloth. Though the material resisted, her other hand held firm with a tireless grasp, keeping the hoop completely immovable.

Audrei exhaled dramatically, but even stern Hildegard could not dampen the mood today. The smile crept back on full lips in a short moment, and she turned again, leaning out the stony frame, eyes staring past the yard and into the streets, over the tops of buildings, straining to soak in the hustle of the all-consuming market square. Though high above, she noticed ladies spilling from a caravan, their dark hair reflecting the sun like polished obsidian. The beautifully ornate visitors, dressed in varying shades of teals and blues as if spilled straight from the depths of the ocean, pulled her in like the undertow of a current. "I wonder what others would make of me if seen from a distance. My blush gown is nowhere near as dreamy as a dress that appeared as if sewn by mermaids of the sea."

A noise escaped Hildegard's throat as a suppressed laugh squeaked out. Over her shoulder, Audrei glanced at her uptight lady, then shrugged, accustomed as she was to the strict personality, and continued both studying and dreaming.

From two carriages, several of the dark maidens stepped onto the streets, straightening their skirts and stretching their weary limbs. "Where do you suppose they have come from?" Audrei asked lightheartedly conspiratorial, as if Hildegard was as enthralled with the possibilities of the outer walls as she. Her eyes remained trained on the fascinating visitors as she waited for the lady's response.

Audrei watched as each visiting young woman embraced the sun, rays stroking their olive skin, but they appeared almost unsure, staying close together. Rising on tiptoes, Audrei swayed side to side, and though her view did not improve from the act, she lifted herself further still.

"Hildegard, please," the princess groaned in a faraway sort of pout, still studying the visitors intensely. "I know you are not interested in such trivial matters, but could you do me the slightest of favors and at least tell me from whence they came?" Cobalt eyes once again glanced over the slight shoulder, and Audrei smiled sweetly but firmly, sugarcoating the direct order.

Now it was Hildegard's turn to sigh as she dutifully lay her needlework down on the small table. Though there were only eight years difference between Hildegard and her mistress, every so often her own twenty-four years felt like a century of difference from the exuberant, carefree princess. Other times, however, the bright, joyful princess with pink rounded cheeks and a smile permanent to her lips allowed Hildegard to feel as though she was one of the youth again.

Sliding delicate hands over her own maroon skirts, brushing the tiny remnants of lint from hours of fine needlework, she relented and stepped to the open window. Easy to pick out in the sea of drab, muted tones, the sight of the beautiful visitors in the city center transformed Hildegard from a reserved lady of the court to a curious debutante. Her own brown eyes lit with intrigue as she leaned forward, soaking in the view. "Oh, I see! They are different, aren't they?"

"See? I told you." Audrei nudged shoulder to shoulder happily. "Where are they from?"

"Well, let's see." Hildegard studied the ladies, then the guards that seemed to be their escort. "Those men look like they're from the south.

The gray uniform is clearly Lōunarike, but the ladies are from somewhere else. They dress more extravagantly than those in the south, and their skin is much darker. I'd say they're from the coast somewhere. Maybe north of here?"

"Really? From the north? Like the Emerald Coast?" Audrei's wide eyes grew with excitement, and her smile wider still. "Could we go into the market today?" she nearly pleaded, clasping her hands together in prayer form. "Please? I'd love to speak to them. I've never spoken to Smarahavie ladies before, and you know that emerald is my favorite color." Half begging, half demanding, the young princess looked to her lady, thick sandy eyebrows a few shades darker than her own golden tresses tilting dramatically upward.

The sight of the girl melted Hildegard's heart, and she stood still for a moment, feeling the warm breeze float in through the open window, kissing her face as a shy autumn embrace. "Your highness," she tried, but her voice caught, torn between duty and friendship. "You know I would follow you anywhere, but the king and queen would never allow you to simply socialize outside these walls. Especially this time of year. You know how affected your mother becomes during these weeks. We celebrate the Lost Prince, but we silently mourn him as well."

Audrei released her breath, held for a surprisingly long time, and her shoulders drooped as she deflated. "Even lost, this brother of mine still ruins my life."

"Oh, sweetie, that's what brothers are for. Even ones that are gone. They're a part of us, and thus bent on making our lives miserable," Hildegard consoled. Reaching out, she brushed a stray golden lock from the soft, royal cheek. "Someday you'll be able to move about, in and out of the walls as you please."

"Is that so?" a sturdy voice called from across the room, calm and collected. Queen Felicity glided across the chamber with grace and dignity, but a shadow loomed overhead as if she awaited dark fate to rob her further. Half her sandy hair was gathered high into beautiful swirling knots, encompassed by her royal crown, while the remaining strands flowed long and straight over her shoulders. "Out of the walls?" she asked with a careful smile. Her soft voice contradicted her rigid posture, exuding an invisible tension.

"Mother," the princess exclaimed quickly. Pink lips immediately smiled with delight, though the joy fell short of her blue eyes. Instead, her pale cheeks blushed as though she were caught sneaking sweets from the kitchen. "Out? No. I mean, well, maybe we might have been sort of discussing the possibility . . ." Audrei wrung her hands as she often did when caught off guard, finally biting her lip to stop the mumbling.

"Your majesty," Hildegard interjected, "Lady Audrei and I were gazing at the marketplace with all the excitement as the days of celebration began. There are so many exciting things happening, so many fine wares, curious and lovely people so far below."

The shadow darkened over the queen. The heartache on her face, even after eighteen years, was heavy this time of year. "Oh, my sweet girl, I'm so sorry." Felicity spoke softly as her fingertips gently caressed her daughter's cheek. "I want you to have everything you have ever dreamed of, you know that . . ."

"Then you'll let me go out with Hildie?" the young dreamer asked prematurely.

". . . but your safety means more to me than anything in the entire world. We don't know who or what is out there, waiting to take advantage of a beautiful lady of royal blood. Once older you'll be able to make decisions for yourself, but until that time, you must obey. Stay inside the castle gates, that's all we ask." The shadow lifted slightly. "You are free to move about anywhere you'd like within the royal estate, converse with visitors and friends, but going out among people we do not know . . . What if someone were to take you too?" Felicity's words caught in her throat, sorrow clouding her face.

Audrei's furrowed brows of frustration smoothed back. Even simply speaking about the loss dredged up old, repressed emotions, and the pain showed with every word. She glided to the queen, gathering her in a brief embrace that grounded the two in solidarity. "Fear not, Mother. I shall yearn to go outside the walls no more."

Hildegard stood back to allow the royal pair a moment, her hands neatly laying on top of each other while her eyes rolled slightly. A knowing smile crept onto her raspberry lips, knowing her mistress's wandering desires were far from quenched.

Felicity backed away from her daughter, closing her eyes and inhaling deeply. When she opened her lids, a slight smile played in her green eyes. Light entered back into her soul, decreasing the shadows to near nothing. "Goodness, I lost track of the hour. I must check in on the arrangements. Walk down with me?"

"I'll be down soon," Audrei replied halfheartedly. Socializing, sampling delicacies, and wearing beautiful day gowns were all Audrei's favorite ways to pass the morning, but her heart wasn't quite in it today.

Felicity felt the conflict radiate from her daughter's glistening eyes and placed a gentle hand back on the side of Audrei's sweet face. "You don't mean the world to us. You *are* our world." The princess smiled softly in reply. With finality, the queen stepped back and headed for the door. "It's not like you're confined to one tower. You have the entire estate to roam. There isn't anything beyond that demands your attention, and nothing we cannot bring to you." Meant to soothe, the words pierced Audrei's already aching heart as Felicity slipped through the chamber doors.

The young ladies left behind stood still for two breaths. Audrei, feeling slightly empty inside, finally glanced toward Hildegard for some sort of guidance. The lady-in-waiting jolted to life, quickly busying herself with pillows on the settee, avoiding the questioning gaze.

Taking the hint, small shoulders slouched ever so slightly as the princess turned back to the window just in time to notice the exotic visitors loading back into their caravan. "Welp, they're leaving," she stated with defeat, resting a small hand on the cool window's ledge. Hildegard halted her busy work to glance at her mistress, feeling the palpable disappointment.

An exaggerated breath flowed in through royal lips, and Audrei held it an extra moment longer, then released with force. Whipping around, her golden hair flew over her shoulders as her she upset her gown in a flurry of pink waves. "I accept my place and responsibilities," she stated matter-of-factly, chin high and brightness in face.

"Yes, my lady." Hildegard quickly nodded, trying to keep up with the varying emotions. "It's good to see you back in your proper spirits."

"Of course, Hilde." The princess's pink lips drew into a beautiful bow, creating envy-worthy cheeks. Flowing over the floor, her steps were soundless in her slippers, as taught since a babe. "I'm happy to obey my mother's commands. It would break my heart to hurt her."

Hildegard swelled with warmth as she smiled at the sweet royal maiden whose heart was as large as her personality. Quickly, she followed her lady's' cue and crossed toward the door as well, the sound of her own slippers deafening in comparison to the petite mistress. Skilled hands grabbed hold of the thick iron handle and pulled just as Audrei continued. "However . . ." The princess stepped through, lowering her voice, and the pair glided down the landing toward the stairs. ". . . the second I see another beautiful lady from Smarahav so close to my palace, wild stallions will not be able to stop me from talking to her."

Hildegard quietly gasped, as if the brazen threat her mistress declared was an unexpected arrow to the back. Somehow, she continued to keep pace. "You wouldn't!"

At the balustrade, the two ladies walked side by side down the wide stairs. "I would." The two words were heavy with a promise, and Audrei planted her feet, forcing Hildegard to stop awkwardly as well. With exasperation, the lady-in-waiting turned to her mistress, meeting misty eyes. "Hilde, I love my parents with all my heart—you know that—but that doesn't mean I don't yearn for more. I'll embroider, read, paint, host parties like a sweet little lamb, but mark my words. If an opportunity falls in my lap, I will not hesitate."

Hildegard's cinnamon eyes widened, then darted around the entrance hall. Satisfied, she settled her nerves and looked straight at her mistress, eyebrows knitted in both sternness and pity. "Then, if you don't mind, my lady, I'm going to pray the opportunity stays at bay."

The radiant smile reappeared on the royal pink lips, and Audrei brushed her sunshine hair back, the thin, delicate crown sitting firmly on top of her golden tresses. "Oh, Hilde! Don't fret. When will I ever get an opportunity like that?" Her blue eyes sparkled with imagination as she continued her descent to the open floor below.

Hildegard delayed, closing her eyes and taking a deep breath. Audrei, her sweet charge, carried the joy and light of the sun in her very soul, overpowering every room with her radiant beams. Exhausting as it was, Hildegard's purpose was to create balance by being the moon, calm and grounded.

9

DOWN THE WALL

Ransom sat back to listen skeptically and then slowly pulled in with curiosity as the tale progressed. Finally, he was leaning forward as far as a body could stretch, eyes wide with complete enthrallment. His focus changed back and forth from the details of the story to the beautiful details of Mel's face while she spoke, both story and features enchanting.

"After hours of wandering, I saw this place and thought that an abandoned tower would be a good place to hide, in case those Lōurnian soldiers were still searching." Her shoulders dropped a little, as if the very act of reliving the last few days through story was just as draining as it had been in real time. "They'll never give up. Their king paid a lot of coin for me, for all of us." Her soft voice trailed off as worry clouded her face. "Oh, I hope at least some of the girls made it out." The air of excitement evaporated, and sadness filled her eyes. For the first time since she left home, Mel began to feel the weight of the emotions crash over her like a tidal wave. Sorrow from the betrayal of her people, worry for the girls she left behind, fear of an unknown future . . . Imelda's head spun, and she leaned forward, resting her forehead on her knees. She was on the verge of breaking down but stopped the tears from flowing. *This is the last thing I can control. I will not cry now.*

With a furrowed brow, Ransom stood and began to pace, hoping the movement would help him to better form a plan. *She hasn't really done anything wrong, so maybe I should release her. But what would become of this girl out in the forest all alone? Would she survive, or would the guards eventually find her? Is this elaborate story even true? If it is, she's been through Stillemäch. She could take me there, and I have her necklace as collateral.*

He abruptly stopped pacing and stepped forward to sit in the chair again. "I have a proposition. You want me to release you, correct?"

Mel glared at him quizzically. "I thought that was obvious."

"Quite. Well, I have a problem as well. I would like to finally leave this tower, travel to the closest city to join the king's cavalry. The only problem is that I've never been there and wouldn't know the way. So here's my proposal: I'll release you on your word that you will guide me to the kingdom of Stillemäch." He paused and waited expectantly.

Mel shook her head. "I can't do that. Nope. No way. There might be Lōurian guards patrolling. They'll see me!"

"Don't worry, we'll be careful," Ransom said casually, adding as an afterthought, "and I'll protect you, of course."

Mel scoffed at the thought of the young man fighting off the hardened soldiers. Yes, muscles were defined all along his arms, and his body looked fit and tight. Even being so tall with broad shoulders, she still thought he was delirious if he believed for a minute that he had a chance against those seasoned killers. "I'm going to need more than that."

He half-smiled in amusement. "How about your necklace?" Her brown eyes instantly appeared bigger as her hands prodded the side of her thick trousers. Ransom continued, "I have no use for it. You guide me to where I need to go, and as soon as we arrive, I'll hand over the necklace. You'll have your freedom and your prize."

Mel straightened, stilling herself for a moment to weigh her options. With a sigh, she realized that there was no other possible way and began to nod a resigned agreement, her spirit broken and beat. Then she perked up curiously. "What do you mean you'd like to finally leave this tower? And earlier you asked if I was here to capture you. Why? Have you really never left this place?"

Ransom stood still, shocked at such a ridiculous question. "Of course I've never left this tower! If you only knew how valuable I am . . ."

"How valuable are you?" she asked, unable to mask the curiosity.

"That's not the point," Ransom responded quickly, trying to stay on task. "I need a guide, and you need your necklace. Have we got a deal?"

Finding courage again, Mel shook her head slowly. "It would be insane for me to just join up with a random stranger that literally attacked me and then tied me up. I don't even know your name!"

"Oh, right! My name. I completely forgot." He stepped forward eagerly and stood in front of Mel, his voice altering with dignity. "My lady, may I introduce myself? My name is Ransom, Lord of the Forest."

That made her smile a bit. "You can't just make up a lordship title, or at least not for the whole forest." Something innocent about the way he presented himself helped her to relax.

"Fine, Ransom the Lonely. No, too sad. How about Ransom, Man of the Tower? Does that suit you? In any case, I'm Ransom. Now that we know each other, Mel, do we have a deal?"

The grin melted from her lips as she contemplated for a moment longer, furrowing her brow slightly. Then, without a word, she nodded once in agreement.

"Excellent!" Ransom walked over to her and pulled one end of the rope, loosening the knot. "Let's go."

Mel unwound the rope, discarding it to the floor, and rubbed her wrists as he freed her ankles.

"Wait, now? I just got here. Can't I rest a bit first?"

"There's no time like the present, Mel," he answered cheerily and then turned serious. "My father will be back tomorrow, and I'd like to cover as much ground as I can. He will be furious when he finds out I've left," Ransom explained, filling a leather satchel with food, a flagon of mulled cider, and the necklace. "Along the way I'd like to forage for wild berries, nuts, mushrooms. Maybe try out a small trap or two to see what kind of critter I can ensnare for supper." The thought of catching his own food, not just having it delivered, made his heart leap with joy. *I'm ready.*

Mel pushed herself to stand, stretching out the kinks in her muscles from sitting so long. Another lightning bolt crashed through her head, and she stilled herself, pressing her fingers to the temples for a moment. "Wow, you sure hit me hard," she said when the pain wore off.

"Yeah, sorry about that. Here, drink this." Ransom handed a separate flagon to Mel, and she hesitated. "Go on, take a swig. It'll help with the headache. Father said it's the best cider in all the land, but I wouldn't know since I've only tried this one kind."

She took a sip, letting the smooth drink run down her throat. Ascertaining the flagon was as advertised, she drank a bit more. The amber liquid was pleasantly complex with a mixture of apple, pear, and tree bark, and a slight floral aftertaste lingered. Taught in the arts of fine drink, Mel agreed with Ransom's father. This was a fine cider. "Your father," Mel began, feeling the pain ease in her head, "why does he want to keep you here?"

Ransom shrugged, still moving about busily. "Overprotective, I guess. Wants to keep me where I'm safe, where he can always look after me, you know?"

"No, I don't," she responded automatically, but stopped herself from going down that road paved in self-pity. Her parents sold her to maintain the life they desired. A father that cared sounded kind of nice right now. "Maybe overprotective, or even just protective, isn't so bad. At least you have someone who loves you."

Grabbing the last supplies, Ransom fastened the bag shut and walked to the window. "Yeah, but there comes a point in a man's life when he must become the protector instead of the protected. It's what I was born to do. Shall we?"

Mel stepped forward, but a wave of self-consciousness held her back. The bulky uniform had a sudden feel of immense weight, and the over-sized boots flopped around her feet. "Uh, this may be an odd request, but do you happen to have any smaller clothing here? I can't wear anything of yours, obviously. It would drown me more than this." Mel gestured to the thick vest and baggy pants. "Perhaps you might have something a little smaller?"

"You know, I think I actually might. Hold on," Ransom said as he rushed down the hall to his own chamber, straight to a trunk in the corner. Flipping the lid, he rifled through the contents quickly, pulling out this and that. Finally satisfied, he gathered the collection in his arms and made his way back to the main tower. "Voila! Attire for the lady. They're not new, but hopefully something will fit a little better. I grabbed a couple sizes from when I was maybe thirteen or so, although the boots are from when I was like ten or eleven." Laying the pile at her feet, he backed away.

Mel glanced at him, astonished and a bit impressed, then bent over the pile to explore the contents. A couple of cream-colored shirts, a few trousers in varying shades of brown, boots (brown again, but in good condition at least), and two vests. She chose a few articles that seemed close to the right size. "I'm definitely not going to win any fashion award," she said a little snippy, then realized her folly as she glanced up at the hovering young man. "But these will be perfect for traveling, and much more comfortable than this uniform. Thank you." Ransom beamed with pride, and Mel noticed how handsome his smile really was. *At least this stranger that's manipulating me is easy to look at. Sweet too, under his tough façade.* "Now, where can a lady change in private?"

He guided her down the long, narrow hall to his chamber and then left quickly. Waiting in the main tower, he busied his hands with unnecessary tidying. The new clothes gifted that morning still sat in a pile, unworn. Looking down at his own garments, he noticed the hem of his pants were a little high, the sleeves of his top a bit too short, and the boots slightly snug. "I guess I should change as well," he mumbled, quickly swapping apparel. Valk clicked her beak in his direction, and he smiled at her. "Might as well start a new adventure with new boots."

Looking sharp, Ransom waited by the table, eyeing the venison that still sat bagged on the table. "This meat is fresh enough to wait a day," he decided, hanging it in a cool spot. Draven wouldn't be happy, but Ransom's focus was elsewhere. Alone in the kitchen, waiting for Mel, a slight tinge of trepidation fell over him. *Am I making a mistake? How can I leave my home and everything I've known? How can I disobey Father after all he's done for me? Why did he say no? Doesn't he want me to be happy? I am a man now, and my own person. It's time to choose for myself.*

"Ah-hem." A throaty sound startled Ransom out of his thoughts, and he turned to see Mel standing behind him, wearing the old clothing. Without the bulk of the thick uniform, the smooth curves of her body were pronounced, and Ransom felt momentarily paralyzed. He swallowed, trying to gain control of his senses, and nodded with a slight smile. "Glad the clothes fit."

"Me too," Mel replied, surveying herself with a hint of satisfaction. "It's not my normal gown with taffeta and boning, but it actually works quite nicely." Reaching up, she combed her hair back with her fingers, gathering the unruly tendrils into a sleek and reserved knot on top of her head. "Okay. I think I'm ready. Let's do it."

With their provisions on Ransom's back, he stepped onto the ledge but paused before lowering down. Mel crawled over the side, grabbed a hold of the thick vine, and began her own descent before noticing her newly acquired companion was not following. "Hey," she hollered up, pausing in her own precarious position. "Are you coming?"

Ransom gazed over the sea of trees, the quaint meadow, and the blue horizon, soaking in the view that had belonged to him alone for too long. *Farewell, lonely tower.* Trepidation still lingered, but adventure beckoned louder. *If I ever see this view again it'll be with new eyes, for I'll be a different man.* He glanced down at the woman hanging below his feet. "I'm ready."

Descending the wall was not nearly as difficult as climbing up had been, and Mel lowered to the ground with some semblance of grace. Feet touched the grass below, then scrambled quickly to the side. He landed with a muted thud onto the disguised platform where she had just stood, and froze, allowing the moment to soak in. For the first time in almost eighteen years, Ransom saw things differently. No longer was he above everything and out of reach. No more standing back and watching from a distance. He was free.

The scents in the air wafted in the breeze, earthy, rich, and sweet. The wind was no more than a breeze, allowing new sounds to reach his ears as insects scattered and hummed underfoot. Even the sun's powerful rays somehow felt different on his skin. Ransom stepped forward, pulling off his gloves, and crouched down to run his fingers in the tall meadow grass. Some of the green blades were flat and wide, hearty and sharp, while others were delicate, bending freely with the slightest touch or wisp of the wind.

Watching the young man as he met the world, Imelda cleared her throat to bring him back to reality. When he didn't immediately respond, she set her course due west and began to walk across the clearing. Snapping back to reality, Ransom followed, but a dandelion caught his eye and he veered to pluck the sunny flower from its broad leaf bed. "It's beautiful," he muttered to himself. Valk swooped down, landing gracefully on the tufts of meadow greenery beside her friend, protective and devoted.

Mel glanced back, then looked toward the forest. *I could run. It wouldn't be too hard. I could wind through the trees and go in a completely different direction until I am in a territory no one could possibly suspect.* She turned back again. *But I need that necklace.* It was the key to her survival, and once it was sold she would be able to buy new clothes, food, and passage back to Smarahav. *I could leave, but I'd have absolutely no security or coin to my name.* She looked back again at the distracted manipulator and groaned. The urge to run was strong, but she fought it. *A deal is a deal. We are in this together now.* "Ransom! Stop," Mel hollered just before he grabbed a purple thistle. "Those have thorns. Really nasty ones, too."

"Oh, you're right. I forgot about that. Thanks. I really don't want to get cut." Instinctively, he pulled the leather gloves back on and stood still, inhaling deeply. "So, which direction are we headed?"

Mel pointed west again. "That way, sir. Do you think you can keep up?" she asked, genuinely curious.

Ransom turned his blue eyes to his guide, peering down at her lovely olive face. She looked excellent in his old clothes. Not fancy like a lady, but the shape of the top complemented her immensely, and the trousers somehow followed the curves of her hips and thighs better than they ever did on his fourteen-year-old self. "Oh, I'll keep up."

"Good. Let's go." Together, they crossed the wide open meadow and entered the dimmer confines of the deep woods.

10

FOREST DWELLERS

"Hey, you're wandering again. Put some of that moss in your pocket and keep walking," Mel called out, half annoyed and half amused. She pushed ahead, dragging him behind on an invisible rope as he explored the new world. Even with all his detours, the pair made their way through the forest briskly. "You know, if you'd stop stopping at every pine cone and toadstool in our path we'd have a better chance of making it to an inn for supper," the young woman shouted over her shoulder, then turned forward. "Maybe we could get some reliable directions while we're at it," she mumbled to herself, not trusting her own orientation.

Ransom shrugged good-naturedly, too enamored with the variety of flora and fauna. "Mel, this is the best day of my life, and you would have me race by," he replied, slowly studying the underside of the forest canopy. He'd seen every one of these trees from the highest viewpoint, but he never envisioned how incredible and intricate they were underneath. The summer sun spilled through tiny cracks here and there, and Ransom stepped into a small pool of light, the rays warming his face. "Soak it in a little, feel the force, the life."

Mel paused her tow, allowing her partner to catch up. "The life?" she responded, kicking dirt his way. "What life? It's just you and me."

"The forest is alive, Mel. Not in a creepy, spooky sort of way. I can feel it, the energy of the trees, as if they confide in one another. Even the ground has a vibration, like the earth itself is a living being. It's hard to explain, but my feet have been on solid stone all my life, and I can just feel the difference. I love being surrounded by life. Smell it," Ransom offered, snapping off a small pine bough and inhaling the strong, sharp fragrance as he meandered past a befuddled Mel.

Mel shook her head in exasperation. "The only scent I want to smell is a warm meal," she called to his back before catching up, then quickly passing. Mel pushed forward while Ransom was all but dragged behind. Though impatient, she gave him a little slack as her understanding grew.

Entranced by the beauty of the wild, he couldn't help but get lost in the music of the thousands of hidden birds in the enormous treetops overhead, or touch every rough trunk and flexible fern, smell the bark, the soil, the flowers. Patiently, she coaxed Ransom from a patch of wonderfully green clover with bright purple blossoms, but other times she had to hastily pry him from a skunk's burrow under a fallen tree. Every once in a while frustration overwhelmed Mel, and she resented their accord, but then there were moments when his childlike awe of the world's splendors made her smile. Excitement and joy were infectious, and, although she still didn't care to hold freshly unearthed grubs or touch the bumps on the underside of an oak leaf, she did find herself noticing the finer details of the forest all around.

Once again, Mel stopped. "Ransom! We're never going to make it anywhere if you keep smelling all the pine cones. One was great, five was plenty, but this has got to be your twentieth at least!"

"Thirty-seventh," he recounted, holding the nubby cone in his hand.

"Well, I would suspect that they all start smelling the same now. Can we please continue?" she called back down the trail with exasperation. The small tapping of her impatient foot barely made any noise in the dirt as she gazed up in a futile effort to track the sun.

"Thirty-eight," Ransom called, dropping another cone behind his back to jog the small distance between them. Sandy hair flew in his face as he stopped beside her and he brushed it back, flashing a broad smile. "Sorry, Mel. There was a beautiful patch of wildflowers back there that distracted me." Swinging his arm up, he offered a token of appreciation. "This is for you." Mel hesitated accepting the wild yellow rose, unsure of what it meant. Ransom saw her uncertainty and his smile grew bigger. He took a half step closer. Without invitation, he reached around, tucking the slender stem into the thong that held her hair up. The sunshine yellow showed even brighter against her thick obsidian hair. "There. I saw a picture of a woman with a flower in her hair once. It looks much better in person, and in color."

"Thank you," was all she could think to say. The sweet moment lingered, and blue eyes locked on brown. She tried to hear what was unspoken as baby butterflies fluttered in her stomach. Snapping back to reality, Mel turned southwest to continue their trek. "Come on," she said, a little softer than before, "we have to keep moving."

Ransom wasn't sure what was shared between them just now, having no experience with the ladies, but he did know that he liked the tough girl fate had brought into his life. She was stronger than she looked, not much different from himself, but her strength came from a will to survive, not magic, which, in his opinion, was much more impressive. Then there were moments like now that showed the sweetness she hid inside. When still, allowing herself to soak in a moment or feel the gentleness of the surroundings, Imelda transformed from beautiful to incredibly stunning. Ransom shook his head, stepped forward to follow, but hesitated when something to the side caught his eye. "Wait, what's that?" he called out, immediately darting off the trail to a group of shrubs under a giant elm.

"Oh, come on! We have to make it to the next town by nightfall so we can buy some supper. I'm not a very good cook on the campfire," Mel shouted back with annoyance. When he did not return right away she looked over to see what had caught his eye. A great heap lay on the leaf- and twig-covered earth. She sighed, then curiously followed.

Ransom approached the lump with caution. It was most likely a wounded animal, but the irregular folds of the hide and the way the poor thing was lying on the earth made identifying the creature extremely difficult. Slowing his steps, he examined it.

"Careful!" Imelda hissed, so close behind that Ransom jumped in surprise. She took a step back as he stepped forward. Nervously, she reached down into her boot and drew her dagger, just in case.

Close enough to touch, he circled the carcass to get a look at the other side, then stopped with surprise. "Mel, come see this. I'm pretty sure it's a woman."

Mel's muscles immediately released their tension, and she slid the knife back into its sleeve. "What? A woman?" Walking around to Ransom, she saw the gnarled face of someone who lived a very long, hard life.

"Check to see if she's dead." Ransom passed it off as a casual suggestion, but he wasn't fooling anyone. This was the first deceased body he had ever seen, and it was not pretty or peaceful.

Mel gave a little huff. "No thanks. Anyone can tell that the poor old gal is gone."

"What do you think killed her?" Ransom asked, a little saddened by the thought.

"Old age, disease, weather, ugliness . . . "

Ransom looked up at Mel curiously. "Ugliness? Why do you say that?"

Mel's cheeks blushed slightly. "Where I'm from, beauty is treasured, and those that are deemed, uh, difficult to look at are rejected and turned out of the city. Some make a home in the forest, but most can't survive the rough."

"Oh, poor woman." Ransom shook his head slowly. "Father always said this was a cruel world, but I didn't think it would be this bad. Poor old, sad woman. So pitiful. Died, all alone, because she was just so very ugly."

"Who you calling dead?" croaked a dry old voice. Cloudy eyes cracked open with effort. Mel and Ransom jumped back, both letting out a shriek of terror, and Ransom quickly coughed, adjusting his shrill pitch two octaves lower. "Now what in the red moon is the meaning of this infernal racketry? Here I be, taking a little interlude in the summer breeze, and then to be set upon by two screeching owls!" The old woman rolled over on to her knees and pushed herself up with immense strain. Leaves clung to the wild gray nest of hair on her head, and her simple homespun dress was covered in smudgings from the forest floor. She dusted the front and back of her skirts, with very little effect, and looked up at her stunned audience. "Well," the disheveled crone questioned, "what do ye two birdies want with a poor ugly biddy such as meself?"

"Well, um, we, well . . . " Ransom stammered, caught off guard. He never imagined meeting a creature so disgusting and fascinating all at the same time, and found it difficult to choose the correct words.

Imelda glanced at her bumbling traveling companion and pity washed over her. She stepped in out of mercy. "Please, madam, our sincerest apologies. We were traveling west and saw you sleeping in the leaves. My friend here gallantly insisted on making sure you were all right, against better advice." She spoke the last words through gritted teeth. Ransom and Mel stood still for a moment while the old woman processed the tale. Even though the story was innocent enough, one never knew how a person, especially a forest dweller, would react.

The cloudy yet alert eyes studied the pair, untrusting, but in the next instant something snapped and the woman's demeanor changed entirely.

"Oh, gallantry, ye say?" she unexpectedly exclaimed. "My oh my, what a lucky damsel I be. What a strapping young man, so kind and attentionly." Doing her best to walk with grace, the old crone sacheted up to Ransom, sliding her arm through his, linking the two together while boxing out Mel. "How would I ever pay ye? Please, young man, come to me home so we can feed ye and show our thanks"

Baffled, all he could mutter was "We?" as he was swept away with no control, caught in an undertow of sorts.

"Oh yes," the woman responded, pulling him closer to her aged body so he could now smell the musty scent of mold and mushrooms. "My sisters and I would love to repay ye for dutifully checking on a poor piti-fullery soul such as meself." They walked a few feet, and then she shouted over her shoulder, "And yous may come along too, deary."

"No thanks," Imelda called back, but her feet move forward despite her reservations. She wondered if she was following unconsciously out of honor and duty, or maybe she just didn't care for the thought of being left all alone. Whatever the case, she made a deal and needed the necklace back, so she would honor that bargain no matter the company.

The old lady kept her prize, guiding him farther off the path, deep into a thickly woods. Despite her age and haggard appearance, the woman walked with a quick step, and Mel tried to keep up from behind. Thin green limbs slapped her in the face, and leaves became entangled in her thick black hair as she struggled on the path that the two in front seemed to slide through easily. Another fifty paces and the trees were so thickly grown that there was barely light from the sun, and too dense to see three feet in any direction. Ransom and the old woman melted into the thicket, and a small sense of panic crept up Mel's back. Pushing leaves out of her face, she stumbled forward, hoping it was the correct direction, with no sight of the two in front. Finally, she thought she understood what Ransom was saying about the forest being alive, and it was terrifying. Closing in, looming, defensive, the trees lost their inviting nature, and panic welled up higher. Her feet tried to move more quickly, only result-ing in sloppy footing and more stumbling.

Something unseen wrapped around her ankle and pulled unexpectedly. Mel fell forward, grasping at young trunks and flexible limbs on her way to the ground. She landed on the dark, leafy floor, catching herself just before her face plowed into the loamy soil. Damp leaves clung to the palms of her hands, wet and cool, but her head was no longer in the darkness of the thick grove. Her hair felt warm from the sun's rays, and Mel nervously glanced up to behold a small clearing with a humble crooked house in the center. Pushing herself up, she plowed through the final feet of the thicket and fully emerged into the bright sunshine and open air.

She paused, trying to orient herself as the backs of Ransom and the biddy were still walking away. "Well, isn't that great," Mel huffed with hands on her hips, feeling completely forgotten. Still scowling, she turned to survey the area. "Where are we?" The words escaped her lips hushed and apprehensive. Unlike Ransom's meadow, this place was not naturally bare, but rather cleared by hand, carved out of the thick surrounding grove. It was obvious that whomever lived here worked hard to create a hidden oasis in the center of the woods. Young green vines and shoots sprung from the ground in short, neat rows on the far side, goats and chickens wandering through the garden and beyond grazing freely. Providing for irrigation and general life, a wellspring sat alone, built up with stones all around and a quaint roof above to protect the life-giving water within. A feeling stirred, and Mel couldn't decide if she would rather take a drink or make a wish.

Contorted and askew, a home stood in the middle of the glade looking completely dilapidated and strangely out of place. Logs shaped the walls, cut to every thickness, some laying vertical while others were horizontal. The hovel widened from a narrow foundation to eaves where the roof flared wildly, swooping to stretch into the sky, curving up into a narrow point. A small stone chimney rested by the side of the pointed center looking as though someone haphazardly stacked random rocks before becoming distracted and failing to finish. Wisps of smoke escaped the center of the contorted chimney. *What could be going on inside a place like this?*

On the doorstep, Ransom glanced back at Mel, as if finally remembering her existence, the old crone still jabbering. Mel tried to act angry for being left behind, but the look on his face made her more curious than bitter. He nodded toward the open door, opening his eyes wide as if to say, *Should we risk it?* Ransom replied to whatever the hag had said, and Mel caught the last of his response, ". . . really should consult with my friend first before committing to anything." He spoke politely, trying to delay. "Ah, Mel, I'm glad you caught up. Our dear friend Nedgie here has invited us to dine with her and her two sisters this eve. What say you?" He gave a slight smile, knowing that Mel would be the one to turn down the old crone.

Somehow, he thinks he already knows me, she thought slyly. *I won't give him the satisfaction.* Instead of declining as expected, she went against her better judgment and accepted the invitation. "Madam . . . "

"Nedgie," the woman croaked at her in correction.

"Nedgie," Mel adjusted, "we would love to dine with you and your sisters."

"This way then," Nedgie grumbled, wiping her bulbous nose, then pointing through the door. She stepped in ahead of the pair, expecting the guests to follow.

Ransom's smile grew a little bigger, and he opened his palm, gesturing toward the open door. "After you." Mel glared at him, then lifted her chin dramatically and stepped over the threshold into the tiny cabin with Ransom trailing after.

Expectations were set so low that anything beyond a couple cut logs for chairs around a small hole-in-the-wall fireplace would have been a surprise, but what was presented before the traveling couple was truly amazing. From outside, the cabin looked barely large enough to hold the old woman and two guests, but inside space seemed limitless. Ransom felt as though they'd stepped into somewhere not of this world, and he had an inkling that his new old friend may be more than a simple forest dwelling peasant. The floor, though made of wood planks as expected, was incredibly smooth and polished to perfection. In the center of the room, a banquet table lined with four carved mahogany chairs on each side sat under a glistening chandelier. The light of two dozen candles spilled over the incredibly crafted furniture and brightened the entire room.

Fire roared in the oversized stone fireplace, and above, on the smooth log wall, hung a painting of three beautiful young ladies. The girl posed in the front appeared shorter than the others, with great big violet eyes and hair as black as Imelda's, but naturally tightly curled. A second girl stood in the back, tall and thin with straight ashy brown hair down to her hips, with the same purple eyes, looking kind and sweet. The third in the picture most likely had identical vivid eyes as the other two, but onlookers would never know with the lids closed. She stood upright, just as the other two, but this girl's chin rested forward on her chest, peaceful in her slumber. Her silky golden brown hair was pulled into an elegant swirl on top of her head.

As Mel studied the three young ladies, Nedgie snuck up from behind. "Sometimes I wish I'd had that painter redo the portrait, and maybe imanginarely put me eyes awake, but nah. That's not me, and it never would be. Ye see, children, I'm narcolepticary and that's just my lot in this here life."

"This was you?" Mel asked, stunned by the toll time had taken.

A second old woman, just an inch shorter than Ransom, came bouncing down a hall that seemed to go as long as the tower. Tall and thin with straight, perfectly white hair braided all the way down to her rear end, she squealed with childlike delight. "You're here! Oh wondrous! We're so very excited to have you, my dears. Guests! Marvelous! Can you believe it, Nedgie?"

"'Course I can believe it. I brought them, didn't I?" Nedgie answered with exasperation. "Mozelle, meet our guests . . . uh . . . "

The young man stepped forward and bowed. "Ransom, madam. And this is Mel."

The young lady shot him a look. "I can speak for myself, thank you."

Everyone ignored Mel's comment as Nedgie started in again with the saved damsel act. "Mozelle, ye shoulda seen it. This here lad came to me rescuing after I fell asleep in the thicketry again. Most would have just wandered by without one thought me way." She gave a small, sharp glance at Mel, then continued her praise. "But not this kindly lad. He's a true gentleman."

From the long hall appeared another woman. "We are indeed grateful that you were so kind to our sister, Ransom." The third sister, shorter than the other two, glided gracefully into the room, bringing with her an air of confidence and control. Her curls were much shorter than the painting depicted, barely grazing her shoulders, and the color had faded to a scattering of salt and pepper. But the violet eyes and the expression on her face were as bold as the day they were painted. "My name is Effie. You've met Nedgie, of course, and this is our sister, Mozelle. Welcome to our home. You've come a long way." She nodded to Ransom, then turned. "And you even longer, Imelda."

Mel immediately tensed. *How does she know my full name?* She looked at Ransom, who mirrored the same confusion. *How were these homely, isolated women expecting us?* The violet eyes waited patiently as the two guests pieced together the puzzle. *Witches.*

11

STEW, STICKS, AND STARS

Shock, tension, fright. Flashbacks of frightening tales from his childhood raced through Ransom's mind, and from the look on Mel's face, he could tell that she grew up listening to similar stories. Immediately, his eyes darted to the small particulars of the home, noticing things that were easily overlooked. In the far corner, shelves lined the wall, holding oddly shaped jars. Some of the contents appeared liquid or gelatinous, and others were more solid, fuzzy, or alive. Underneath were a few wider shelves for mortars and pestles, bowls, utensils of all shapes and uses, and more pots for brewing. Hanging on the wall were several bouquets tied together and turned upside down. They were now dry and brittle. *What kinds of potions were these prepped to concoct?*

Through an open doorway into the study, Ransom saw a large desk covered in a variety of intricate brass tools. He couldn't identify all of them from where he stood, but he recognized a miniature telescope propped on a tripod, as well as a shiny astrolabe. Behind the desk, stars were painted on the wall in intricate patterns. *Most likely as a way to tell the future and see the past.*

A long leather carrier lay unrolled on the banquet table. Pockets lined the delicately made wrap, and peeking out were several wooden handles of different sized knives, blades hiding inside their leather slots. Lying on the table was a small blade, thicker than Imelda's dagger, but half the length, and a file for sharpening. A hatchet, wedge, and mallet were also close by. *Torture.*

In the massive fireplace, an enormous cauldron sat in the middle of the blazing fire, no doubt where the three sisters intended on placing

Ransom and Mel before supper as the final ingredient. Flames licked the thick black cast iron, and although the scent escaping was rich and tantalizing, Ransom's stomach turned sick. Without playing coy, he spoke his final thought out loud. "I mean no offense, but please tell me you're not witches," he said, hoping he had deduced incorrectly.

Effie studied the faces of Ransom and Mel as they came to a full understanding of their current predicament. "Oh, my dear children. Please, sit down a while. We have so many things to discuss, and there's much you don't yet know."

"No." Mel stepped forward, shaking but strong. "We won't be sitting anywhere. If you'll pardon us, we must be on our way." She started to the door.

Mozelle stepped forward, covering the length of the room quickly on her long legs, and positioned herself in front of the exit. "I'm so very, very sorry, my dears, but we're not ready to let you go yet."

Ransom looked at Mel, and a powerful feeling took over. He turned to Effie, the smallest but obviously the one in charge, and spoke clearly. "Please, you can have me. Let Mel go and I won't fight you."

"Ransom, no!" Mel responded instinctively. Fear destroyed all reservations, and she realized she actually liked the boy. He'd been nothing but kind and courteous to her, since . . . well, since the smack over the head with the club. They were basically strangers, but somehow he had already become the best friend she had ever had. "I won't leave you here. If these witches want to kill one of us, they'll have to kill both of us."

Ransom turned to look at Mel, ignoring the rest. "It's all right," he said softly, "this is my destiny. I was born to save the innocent and free them from the wicked. If your life is the only one I save, I could die happily."

"Destinedly, ye say?" Nedgie piped up, looking like she could use another nap. She plopped in a dining chair and settled herself before continuing. "Lad, you were not destined to die with us withery women today. We have no interest . . . " Mid-sentence, the crone's eyes shut, and her body slumped forward onto the glossy table.

Effie stepped in, picking up where her sister had left off. "We have no interest in killing you," she said, looking proud. "Either of you."

"Then what is all this? The elements for potions." Ransom pointed to the room through the doorway. "The star divination, the display of knives?" He gestured toward the table with skepticism in his voice.

"Oh, those are mine!" Mozelle called out happily from her position by the door.

Effie smiled at her long, sweet sister, then turned back to their guests. "Some are destined for greatness, young man, and some are destined for ordinarily extraordinary things. Mozelle had always wanted to be a . . . "

"Woodcarver!" Mozelle burst out excitedly. "I just love carving. Have you ever tried it? I feel such a connectionary to the wood. It speaks to me, you know, like it's what I'm meant to do." The guests couldn't help but smile at the overexcited woman. "I don't know how to explain exactly. Something magical happens when I simply touch, talk, or think about pine, oak, and maple. To shave off the bark, cut into the soft, springly core of a young one, and smooth out the rough edges . . . "

Ransom glanced at the table. "So this arsenal of weapons, these knives and blades, they're yours?"

"Weapons? Yes, yes they're mine. But, silly dear, they're tools, not weaponaries!" Mozelle stepped forward with excitement and adoration, leaving her post in front of the door. "Ye see, children, these are my most preciously possessions." Her fingers rested lightly on top of her open leather roll. The mood shifted dramatically, and a tear came to her eye.

No longer blocked, Mel inched her way to the exit, but Ransom, moved by the tear, stepped toward the tall old woman. "If you love it so much, why do you cry?"

Effie was the one to answer, gentle but protective of her sister. "Two lefty thumbs. She can't hold the toolery tight enough to carve anymore. As time has passed, her thumbs have become more and more crookedness. Now, she can hardly pick anything up at all." Effie walked up to her sister, who was quite a bit taller, and rested her hand high on Mozelle's shoulder. "Imagine how painly and torture-like it be to know what you're meant to do and not be able to do it. Downright misery."

Mel reached the door, but her friend didn't follow. "I have an idea," Ransom said with empathy, looking at the delicate but gnarled hands of the sweet sister.

"Like reaching a door you're supposed to go through, but not being able to leave?" Mel pointed out sarcastically.

"Exactly," Effie stated pointedly, looking over the obvious note of bitterness in Mel's tone. "We all have things we feel we're meant to accomplish in this life, but blockaderies and obstacles arise timely. Just take a look at our poor Nedgie." In response, all eyes turned to rest on the sleeping hag. "She wants, more than anything, to be a chef. Our poor Nedgie loves to cook, and she's fantastical at it! Oh, moonbeams! We would be much roundlier if it weren't for her narcolepticrie. Cooking must be timed and precisely, ye know, and fallin' asleep here and there makes for burned cakes and scorched potatoes."

Mozelle perked up at this, relieved to speak of something that pained her own heart less. "Oh, yes, our poor Nedgie. That reminds me, I'll check on the stew for tonight." Mozelle strode to the enormous fireplace and swung the cauldron out of the blaze. Picking up a wooden paddle the length of her arm, she dipped into the boiling hash with care. Over her shoulder she continued cheerily, "We concocted it while our sister was out, not knowingly when she'd be back and all, so this batch has yet to be burned. For desserts we have a delectablary plum cake that has only been slightly charred on the edges!"

While Mozelle went on about supper plans, Ransom's eyes wandered to the wall of odd-shaped jars and stranger substances inside. Effie studied his face, trying to read the thoughts before they were spoken. "Yes, some of those dobbles and nobbins are used for potions, but the majority of those jars contain seasonings. Ingredientry for our aspirant chef."

"What about the divination? Do you look at futures, or try and change your own?" Mel asked, slowly softening toward the hostesses. "Do you manipulate others into doing as you please?"

Mozelle gave a short snort of a laugh, and Effie turned to study the young, dark beauty. "My dear, I only wish we had that kind of talentry between us, but alas we are not so forceful with the wills of others." She turned back to Ransom and continued. "I am an astronomer, born to map the starlets and search for planetarys. I have devoted my life to the heavens. Sadly, that chapter is coming to a close. My vision, you see, is diminishing rapid-like. Distance is fading from my capabilities, and soon the stars will be a memorary." There was a lull in the conversation where only the sound of crackling embers and heavy breathing could be heard as the two conscious sisters allowed the guests to process.

Complete and total empathy overwhelmed Ransom as he looked at the three isolated sisters. If anyone understood the agony of living with a barred destiny, it was he. He knew the pain of knowing you were capable of so much more, but locked away, whether by key or by ailment. Mel, on the other hand, was not so easily persuaded. All her life she had been told her purpose, never being allowed the luxury of choice. She had been born to serve and to be used as a commodity. There was no greater honor, she was told, and there was no other life. To choose a destiny, to forge ahead and make her own, was a completely foreign concept that she, until this very day, had never considered a real possibility. Though desperately trying to forge her own path, the poisonous mindset of thralldom was hard to squelch when she'd lived obediently for so long. Confused and uncertain, Mel asked what they were both thinking. "Why are you telling us all this?"

"To show you that just because we was born as witches doesn't mean we must be witchedly. We choose our own paths, our own destinies, and no one can take that from us. Beyond that, we are kindred spirits, my dear. You both have incredible destinies that will benefit thousands of lives beyond your own. We may not be able to do anything about our own impairities, but we can help you," Effie stated, standing as tall and proud as her small frame would allow.

Ransom interjected, "But how do you know what we are destined for? Or even capable of? You said those charts were for astronomy."

"Just because we don't use the stars to change others' paths doesn't mean we don't do a bit of dabblery every now and again in the divine." Effie smiled sheepishly at Ransom, then turned to Mel. "Please, would you stay for supper? Give three lonely sisters some company?"

Mel looked to Ransom but received no answer from the look on his face. Instead, he waited to hear her response. His eyes simply said, *If you want to go, I will go, no questions asked. If you want to stay, I will stay.* She could see the choice was all hers. "Promise you won't carve a bewitched wooden doll to look like me and make me do your bidding?" she responded, looking over at Mozelle.

The tall woman's eyes widened with delight. "I promise, by the moon's light, I will not carve a doll of you." Mozelle bounced with glee at the thought of having company for the evening. "Besides," she added off-handedly, "that hair would be way too difficult. I'd just carve one of him."

12

BY THE STARLIGHT

Ransom and Imelda accepted the sisters' dinner invitation, which, they confirmed, did not have their names written on the menu. Instead, Nedgie woke up long enough to add an array of roasted ground squirrel, acorn mushroom stuffing, porcupine pie, wood snake pâté on barley cracker-bread, along with sautéed wild squash and boiled sweet pumpkin to accompany the thick, rich badger stew. The entrées were out of the ordinary but surprisingly delectable. Both guests, though hesitant at first, dug in hungrily when they realize their ragged old friend could actually make a fricassee as good as they claimed.

Baking confectioneries was an art only few had mastered, and gruff old Nedgie was numbered among the elite. Her rhubarb, blackberry, and rosemary pastries were perfectly flaky thanks to the goat's butter and cream, and the red currant berry pudding with wild honey drizzle had the perfect balance of sweet and tart. Finishing off the meal, carrot cordial made for a slightly sweet and deeply earthy thirst quencher to wash it all down.

Effie, dignified and poised, tried to respectably discuss all the appropriate topics of weather, travel, current marketable goods, and so on. Mozelle, unable to reign in her excitement, inadvertently took the lead on the conversation, and no topic was off limits. Though some questions were a little more probing than etiquette allowed, both Ransom and Mel found themselves enjoying the lighthearted and deep-diving topics, allowing them all to just be real. Halfway through the delectable dinner, Nedgie nodded off, landing her cheek on a loaf of sponge barley bread, and slept through the rest of the meal contentedly.

Hours later, dawn began to set in. Reluctantly, the guests moved to leave before darkness overpowered the sun. "Thank you," Mel barely managed to squeak as Mozelle gave her an exuberant hug goodbye.

"Oh, my dear, I am just so verily happy to have made your acquaintancy." Mozelle beamed. The embrace lasted well over the standard appropriate time limit, and though completely out of her comfort zone, Mel surprised herself by leaning in and squeezing a little tighter than usual. Mozelle pushed her back quickly, gave one more meaningful look, and popped over to Ransom to bestow an equal amount of love.

Effie walked up in her sister's exuberant wake and nodded her head with decorum. Mozelle released her hold on Ransom and stepped back, allowing the calmer sister to have a chance to speak. Effie held a small parcel out for Mel to take, wrapped in a simple linen cloth, and a leather bag for Ransom. "Provisions for tomorrow, and warmth for tonight." She nodded toward Mel's hands, making her salt and pepper curls bounce. "And this. It will help lead you where you're meant to go." Effie stepped forward and gave Mel a small kiss on the cheek, raising herself on tiptoes to do so. The wise sister swiveled to face Ransom and offered an identical peck, but this time with him bowing quite the distance for her to reach. "We have enjoyed you immensingly! Now, go on your way before the moon rises."

Mel nodded her head, choked with emotion from the kindness they had been shown. "I'm not ready to go," she whispered, so overcome with emotion that words felt flat and dry. Despite her feelings, she moved toward the exit. She had never before experienced people so flawed and yet so perfect. *This is what home should feel like*, she thought as she walked out the crooked door.

"Thank you," Ransom said with a sweet, warm smile, then turned to follow his companion out.

"Goodbye!" Mozelle called from behind. "I hope we see each other again!"

Ransom spun around. "Soon!" he called back, but the house was gone and the clearing was empty. Somehow, the sudden disappearance of a house and the people in it didn't faze him in the least. "Soon," he repeated to himself, then turned around and followed Mel back through the thick, uncooperative brush.

✳ ✳ ✳

"Ransom, I can barely see without the sun. Would you mind if we stopped now?" Mel asked over her shoulder as the two trudged through the darkening forest. She stopped and waited.

The eager young man quickened his pace and caught up within a few strides, halting beside the toughened beauty, and scanned their surroundings. "Too bad. I was looking forward to arriving at the city sooner than later."

Mel let out a short laugh. "Are you serious? We still have another full day before we get there, but, with luck, we should be able to make it to the gates before the next nightfall."

Ransom groaned dramatically, then sighed with resignation. "I've waited my whole life. I guess I can handle one more day." With that, he stepped through some trees and stumbled upon an area suitable for camp, Mel following closely behind. They lay their cargo down on the leaves, then began creating a place to sleep. Ransom looked around. "I'll gather wood for the fire. Could you clear a place and make a pit?"

"Of course I can," Mel responded with a tinge of offense in her voice.

Luckily, Ransom was not completely familiar with female dialect and heard the words without any negative inflection. "Great! I'll be back." He took off into the dimming forest.

After a bit of pacing around, Mel placed a few rocks in a circle and called it a pit. With her chore finished and nothing more to do, she sat in the grass to wait. "Huh," she exclaimed softly, feeling a bump in her thigh. Curiously, Mel reached into her pocket, retrieving the small package Effie had given her. "Oh! I forgot all about this," she spoke to herself. Carefully, she unwrapped the thin linen cloth and let out a small gasp. In her dainty hand she beheld the most intricately crafted wooden cage, barely the size and roundness of a hazelnut, with tiny slats spiraling as they bowed out roundly from top to bottom. Looking closer between the slats, she could see another smaller cage made of what appeared to be dried lavender stems. Mel sniffed through the wood, trying to identify the plant that made up this woven orb. It wasn't lavender. It was rosemary stems, from one of the plants that hung in Nedgie's arsenal of culinary herbs. In the depths of the double cage, a tiny speck was suspended in the center, barely visible. No matter which way she turned the cage, the little dust speck floated equidistant from all sides.

Mesmerized, Mel called out half-heartedly, "Hey, this thing is incredible. Come look!" When no one responded, she peeled her eyes away from the awesome trinket long enough to scan the small campsite. "Ransom!" Her voice fell flat in the empty forest. Rocking up to stand, the delicate cage still in her open palms, she took two steps to the left. "No, that doesn't feel right. I think he went the other way," she mumbled to herself, turning back. Three steps to the right and the minuscule speck inside the little double cage looked as though it had begun to glow. "Whoa, is that glowing? Or am I just really tired?" Mel took two more steps to the right, and the speck became slightly more vivid. "Ransom! Where are you?" she shouted, entering further into the darkness, her palm lighting up brighter with each step.

Mel continued wandering, all the time staring at the increasing light as she stepped around tree trunks and dodged low bushes. The brilliance of the tiny speck was enchanting, making it nearly impossible to look away. Smack!

"Ooof! Hey what the—?" Ransom asked as the pile of wood jumped from his arms, falling on his feet and scattering all around. "Mel! What are you . . . "

Running into Ransom's back interrupted Mel's concentration, and she barely caught herself before falling backward. Quickly, she cupped the miniature cage, enfolding it in the cushioned confines of linen, then looked up at her blockade with exasperation. "Careful!" The word flew out as she snapped from the trance with all her thoughts surrounding the preservation of the incredible little object. In the next moment Mel remembered why she was wandering in the first place. "Oh hey. I was looking for you."

"Well, you found me," Ransom responded lightheartedly as he began to regather his bundle. "What's going on?"

"What did the witches—I mean sisters—say about the little bundle they gave us?" Mel asked excitedly.

Ransom paused, confused by the unexpected topic. "They said that it would help lead us where we're meant to go. Why?" Then he noticed the bundle in her hand. "What's in there?"

Mel unfolded the cloth carefully, and the delicate cage rested, unlit, in the palm of her hand.

The dim light didn't help, but Ransom's eyes were sharp enough to see something incredible. He bent to study the object, obviously impressed by the craftsmanship. "Incredible! Mozelle really does have a talent, doesn't she? I've never seen wood carved this precisely." He reached out cautiously, and with the slightest of touches felt the bowed spirals.

"Do you see inside?" Mel asked, once again absorbed in the beauty of the object. "There's a second cage made of rosemary stems. It's barely large enough to hold a jewel."

Ransom looked closer. "I see it. That's amazing!" Gold, yellows, and streaks of bronze caught tiny beams of early moonlight as Ransom's head bent over the thoughtful gift. For a moment, Mel was once again lost in a trance of sorts, thinking of how smooth his hair flowed over his ears, but shook herself back to reality, desperately hoping her absent mind hadn't been noticed.

"Wow," Ransom said in complete awe, "how long do you think it took Mozelle and Nedgie to create this . . . whatever it is?"

Mel shrugged. "Something like this had to have taken months to create, wouldn't you think? There's one more thing."

Ransom continued studying the cage. "I don't see anything else. Are you talking about the tiny little, uh, floating dirt in the middle?"

"Yes! Although, it was much more impressive a second ago. It started glowing. I don't know how or why."

Ransom looked up at Mel with wide eyes. "Really?" He turned back to the perfectly shaped object. "Glowing, huh?" Then a wide smile spread across his face. "Effie! You sly girl. She told me that she'd like to train all the stars in the heavens to show us the way. Then she chuckled and said one would have to do. I had no idea what she was saying at the time, but now I think that maybe I do." Ransom looked back up at Mel to see if she was following his line of thought. "It's a star."

Instead of being skeptical, Mel tilted her head in thought, then nodded in agreement. "That would explain how bright it was getting."

"It's not shining anymore. What changed?" Ransom asked as he peeled himself away from the incredible trinket and began picking up his load of sticks once more.

Mel shrugged and folded the cloth over their new treasure. "Maybe it got scared when I ran into you. Do stars get scared?"

"I dunno. Never had one before. Come on, let's go finish making a fire for the night. I'm really excited to try sleeping on the ground for the first time." With that he began to lead the way back.

Once the tiny orb was safely tucked away, she looked up to see Ransom carrying an enormous load of logs. "Hey," she yelled after him, scrambling to catch up from behind. "Can I help carry some of those? That's gotta be way too heavy!"

"Nah, I got it," he responded, speaking evenly, as if the giant pile required no effort at all. "It's all in the wrists. I'm actually stronger than I look."

"Sure you are," Mel threw back. Though doubtful on the outside, she admitted to herself that she was actually a little in awe. *He may have taken on more than he should be able to carry,* she thought, *but he's doing a great job with it.* No bragging, grunting, or stumbling, he continued to impress, and a half-smile pulled her full lips to the right as she trailed behind the young man.

Back at their little campsite, Ransom stacked the wood, reconfigured the pit, and proceeded to create a fire. Lifting the bag from the sisters, he pulled out two thin blankets, one for each of them. Underneath, in the bottom of the leather bag, parcels of food were wrapped and waiting to feed the couple in the morning. Useless, Imelda sat beside the fire and watched him work through the flames, grateful for light. Ransom moved busily, retrieving water from the little stream about thirty yards south, stoking the fire, collecting kindling, clearing the area of rocks, and so on. After lining a few more stones around the fire, he looked up from across the pit. "So, what does a Queen's Jewel do?" he asked, breaking the silence, looking her way. Tiny orange and yellow dancers swayed across his piercing eyes.

Mel stared at the small pools of fiery blue with her defenses up, searching for meaning and expecting acrimony, but instead she saw genuine curiosity. "Our job was to be on display," she answered, a little shorter than intended. Quickly she continued, working to soften her tone. "We, the Queen's Jewels, live to wait on the Queen's every whim. I was taught to walk gracefully without making any sound. I can embroider the most delicate lace onto fine silk. I was taught the proper wine, food, and dessert pairings, portions, and placements. I can strum the harp softly to accompany a song bird in spring, and I know all the latest dances." Stopping, the proud look faded from her face. "While I looked after the queen all my life, others took care of me. I never learned the basics, like how to cook or clean. I've never built a fire before, or even dressed myself. I used to stand on the balcony and watch the men train for combat, and that's the only way I was able to learn anything about fighting." Mel chuckled to herself. "I can tell you which tea pairs best with which type of scone for brunch, and the historical origin of the tea, but don't ask me how to boil the water unless you want to be very disappointed."

Pushing himself off the ground, Ransom dusted himself off and walked around to Mel. Without asking, he lowered by her side. "All my life I was taught the basics so I could take care of myself, alone in that tower. I can cook, bake, sew a button, or scrub the floor so completely that you would have no problem licking it, but I have never been taught dancing, or etiquette, or really anything a gentleman should know. I was never even supposed to know life was different beyond the tower, but books have a way of bringing the unknown to your feet."

Questions rolled in her head, and one popped into her mind: *What was it like growing up in a tower so high, never being able to experience the real world?* Before she could ask, however, she already had the answer. Mel hadn't been raised in the highest tower, alone without a soul to talk to, but she had been raised on a pedestal, never allowed to speak her true feelings out loud, and with no true friend in which to confide. In an instance, curiosity morphed into camaraderie, and Mel felt as though she knew this stranger more intimately than she'd ever known anyone. Instead of asking questions, she simply proposed an idea. "Let's trade. You teach me basics of survival, and I'll teach you the extras that separate the peasants from the lords."

He turned to face her, eyebrows slightly furrowed as if in deep thought. After a second, they popped up in amiable agreement as he nodded. "Deal." Ransom put out his gloved hand and waited for her to take it as a symbol of an accord.

She reached forward deliberately, keeping her large, dark eyes trained on his lighter baby blues. That half-smile edged on the corner of his mouth again, and she couldn't help but mirror the grin. "All right. Deal," she stated as small fingers slipped around the larger hand.

"Excellent," he said, leaning forward almost conspiratorially, "but first, we dance!" Pushing up quickly, he never let go as he pulled her to stand in a flash. Face to face with the fire in their peripheral, Ransom smiled wide, making Imelda laugh. His tall frame stood solid in front of her, and though he looked thick and smooth as a marble statue, he moved at the slightest touch of her delicate hands. Eager to learn, he bowed as directed, stepped when told, and held her waist lightly when given the command. She studied him while she taught, relaxing with every turn and dropping her guard with every sway, eventually realizing that she was enjoying herself as much as he was.

They danced for a while as the stars began to peek through the darkening sky, one by one, and while entranced in the music-less dance, the forest settled for the night. Their little camp surrounded by trees felt a million miles from anyone else on earth. Lighthearted banter filled the air as they talked about superficial things, not wanting to sully the pleasant night. Tomorrow there would be plenty of time for seriousness, but tonight two strangers were becoming friends.

Long after the glow of the fire dimmed low, red embers pulsing with heat, Ransom and Mel still teased and laughed, enjoying each other's company. A few feet behind, in the leather bag, wrapped in layers of linen, the star in the incredibly crafted cage shone blindingly incandescent.

13

HIDDEN IN THORNS

"Ransom!" The hoarse voice drifted up without reception. "Ransom! Pull me up!" Draven waited only a moment longer before shouting again. "Ransom!" *Something's wrong. The boy may be lazy some days, but he has never refused an order before. What has happened?* Panic bloomed from the pit of his stomach, and Draven worked hard to squelch it while thinking fast. "Ransom!" he shouted in final desperation. Nothing.

Risking everything, he ran to the east tower, scrambled around the rear, and bent back the thick, thorny branches of a wild, overgrown currant bush. Heavy with tiny scarlet fruit among the deep green leaves, the guardian plant was tall and wide, reaching across half the stone wall, though the area it was meant to cover was much smaller. The long, spiny boughs condensed thickly over an old, splintered door, weathered and worn from years of neglect.

Draven struggled to plow through the long, thin boughs as thorns snagged his impeccable clothing here and there. Finally far enough inside the assaulting shrub to reach the hidden door, he lifted the old latch and pushed. "Drat!" Nothing happened. The old hinges refused to give way, fused with age, rust, and lack of use. No longer heeding the bush's angry limbs, he threw himself into the midst of the thorns, ramming his shoulder into the door. In response to his immense effort, the old blockade barely moved at all. Again, Draven pulled back and slammed his body into the stout door. Like a guard that had been given the order to back down by his captain, the heavy wooden sentinel reluctantly crept in. His shoulder throbbed with pain from the wild blows, but luckily he had enough youth left to heal quickly. Another heave and an opening was created, wide enough to slither through.

Inside, a winding staircase began almost immediately, spiraling upwards to the floor of the east tower where Ransom's chamber lay. Draven hurled himself on the dark steps, trusting his feet to take two at a time as he raced to the top, submerging himself in the nearly pitch black corridor. Small slits of light spilled through the walls here and there, allowing him to keep going, as the sun pressed through holes in the sides of the curved tower, carved through the thick stone purposefully.

Finally, the concerned father reached the top of the steps, sweaty and gasping, and immediately pushed firmly above his head. "Come on." Draven coaxed the hidden door, as if words would persuade it to relent. With more push and strain, the thick wooden square creaked from the frame it had been resting in for decades. Relieved, the man slid the plank sideways, raised his head through the hole, and scanned the area. Mostly blocked by the large bed frame overhead, even without seeing, Draven could feel the stillness in the room.

Quickly, he pulled himself up, sliding forward until his body was out of the hole, then rolled to the side and rose to his feet. There, on the floor in a crumpled heap, were unfamiliar clothes. Draven lifted the first article. *A guard's uniform? Lóurnian.* A new kind of fear washed over him, and he dropped the uniform, racing down the hall, scanning the area as he went. "Ransom," he called again, but all he heard was the mocking silence as entered the west tower. "Where are you, boy?"

Desperately, Draven scanned the scene, first noticing the venison hanging in sacks, not drying on racks. *Ransom never shirks his duties, especially when it comes to wasting precious provisions.* But that was not the only thing awry. Food and other items were missing. Cider, bread, and honey were all taken from the stores. Draven turned, noticing another heap of discarded clothes and a rope unceremoniously dropped on the floor. He stepped forward, scooping up the thin cord, and a nervous chuckle escaped his dry lips as he realized that he purchased this rope from the same peddler that led him to his pride and joy, that poppy flower.

What happened here? Did a Lóurian soldier take him? No, Ransom has the strength of a mountain coursing through his veins, as well as years of practical training and rigorous study. If he had been threatened by one worthless soldier, the man would have been dealt with quickly and efficiently. The only other option was that Ransom left of his own volition. This idea ignited fury.

How could he? After all I've done for him! I raised the boy, fed him, provided all that he ever wanted. How could he betray me like this?

"He won't get away with this," Draven snarled. *I'll find him. Somehow.* "Where?" That question was easily answered. Yesterday morning the lad had asked for permission to join the royal cavalry. Instantly, the color drained from his skin. "He met a soldier somehow, that must be it. The two joined together, traveling to Lôunarike." *This cannot happen. It will not happen. He's only been gone one day. How far could an ignorant boy get? He has no one except this mystery guard, and almost nothing to his name.* Draven knew back trails and how to survive in the forest, as well as the quickest route to most places. *With luck, I'll be able to catch the pair before nightfall.* It would be difficult—the forest was ever changing—and so far he only had theories to rely on. But it was enough to propel into action.

Turning back, he raced down the hall, reaching the bedchamber. Panting, Draven lay on the stone floor and rolled underneath the bed, slipping into the dank staircase again. He reached the bottom step, quick but cautious, and slid through the gap in the old, weathered door, yanking it shut behind him. The sharp pain of a pulled muscle served as a reminder that youth was leaving his body at a rapid rate. Panic rose as the feel of his face loosened, wrinkles deepening from the corners of his eyes and across his forehead. *I must have lost ten years already.*

Pushing carelessly through the currant bush, heedless of the snagging boughs, he emerged into the open meadow and scanned the area slowly. With a sigh of frustration, he kicked at a tuft of thick grass. "Not one sign to follow," he griped, willing tracks to appear. "I guess I'll have to rely on instinct for now." Draven turned southwest, where the road between Lôunarike and Stillemäch awaited far beyond the thick wall of forestry. He stepped with purpose, careful but urgent, surveying clearing like a hawk on the prowl.

With a hunter's instinct, Draven paced the edge of the forest in all directions. Ready to give up, he turned, but a light imprint in the dirt begged for a second look. "Aha!" he exclaimed, focusing on the partial boot print pressed in the dry ground, barely noticeable as the perpetrator stepped lightly from the grassy meadow onto the patchy forest floor.

There, beside another longer set of prints showed deeper, heavier. *I was right.* Quickly, Draven turned back toward the tower to retrieve his old mule who was pleasantly grazing, completely oblivious. The beast gave a small grumbled protest deep in his throat, but followed obediently without choice.

Together, the pair slipped into the forest and began picking up the pace, encouraged by his discovery. "Let's move quickly," the aging man spoke to his four-legged companion. "I will find, and kill, the accomplice if I have to, but one way or another Ransom will come home tonight."

14

LADY AND THE TRAP

Thousands of green, hearty leaves swished high above in the early dawn light. Chartreuse, jade, and sage spattered the view above, while patches of gray-blue sky peeked through the lush canopy in tiny, well-hidden pieces. Though early, the birds fluttered and tweeted, already hard at work as they hopped from one branch to another, welcoming the new day. Long lashes bent against cheekbones as Mel squeezed her eyes shut again, but there was no stopping the charging sun. It was approaching, ready or not.

"Morning, Mel." A voice from somewhere high broke the monotony of musical twittering. Peeling her eyes open, she turned her head slightly and was greeted by a broad grin and bright eyes high over head in an enormous oak.

"Ugh. It is way too early. What were you doing up there?" she groaned, rolling over onto her side and pushing herself up to sit. Thick hair, now untied and loose, fell over her shoulders in massive wild waves decorated with twigs and bits of leaves. Gathering the unruly mane to one side, she began to pick the adornments out quickly. Behind, the sound of scraping and shaking could be heard, starting high and gradually getting lower. Finally, a controlled thud thumped the hard earth as two confident feet landed solidly on the ground. "What are you doing up there?" Mel repeated the same question again before he could answer.

"Just taking in the view. I love to wake with the sun every morning, and even though I can't see the horizon from here, I thought it'd be wonderful being around the birds as they wake one by one. I was never close enough to the forest to hear their flutterings or watch them hop from tree to tree." Ransom interrupted himself by making a small *tsk* sound of greeting to his falcon, who landed loyally at Ransom's feet. "I was only able to see the birds that were in flight, or the tiny ones that sat in the tower's vines. They were so busy. Oh look, a squirrel!"

Despite the chilly air and cramp in her neck, Mel began looking at the world through the same rose-colored glasses. He was right. The morning was lovely and lively as all the creatures emerged from their burrows and nests to begin their chores. A smile bloomed on her face despite herself, and Mel conceded. "It really is beautiful," she agreed with reverence. "Now, how about some of that breakfast Nedgie promised us?"

They dug into the leather bag and pulled out a parcel of ginger biscuits, slightly sweetened to cut the zing of the root, a cloth of goat cheese curds, and blackberry beet juice. Again, the food was extraordinary. With the day heating up pleasantly and the chill of the night wearing off quickly, they decided against a morning fire so they could begin their trek as soon as possible. "You reckon we'll get there before nightfall today?" Ransom asked before taking a swig of juice.

She swallowed her last bite of ginger biscuit. "Oh yeah. Easy. As long as there are no real hangups—and I don't foresee any—we should arrive with plenty of time to find a decent place to stay."

Ransom smiled. "I can't wait. All those people. I can only imagine."

Ransom's words struck a chord, and Mel had a sudden feeling of self-consciousness creep up on her. Not sure if it was the thought of seeing real people in the city soon, or just the closeness of the handsome man beside her, but something shifted and she felt utterly embarrassed for her appearance. Quickly, she grabbed a thick twig, picking through the gnarls in her hair, then attempted to straighten the wrinkles in her shirt and dust off her trousers. "I'm so glad I'm not in my gowns on this little adventure, thanks for that, but I am a mess. Is it all right if I at least clean my face at the stream before we go?"

Ransom chuckled a bit, fascinated with the customs and maintenance of the female species. "Go ahead, my lady," he said with a slight bow, a smirk playing on his face. "I'll pack up while you're primping so we may continue our journey when you return."

Mel picked herself up. "Fine with me," she said, glaring back at him over her shoulder, but facing forward she couldn't stop smiling. Walking slowly, she took a moment to admire the incredible tapestry of the forest. Mel consciously tried to take a page from Ransom's book, smelling the sap and noticing the varying shades of brown on the bark. When sprinting for her life, or riding through in a closed carriage, she tended to miss seeing the subtle beauties of the wooded area, as well as the feel of the vibration of life.

The thin, shallow stream trickled merrily by as Mel knelt beside the flowing water. She stared into the ripples, trying to catch a glimpse of the mess that was her reflection, but found it difficult to make out the features of her face. However, the outline of wild, frizzy hair told her, more or less, what she needed to know. "First I'll deal with this mess. Then I'll worry about the rest," she mumbled, angry at herself for allowing her hair to become so unruly. Using her fingers, she untangled the largest knots, smoothing out a little at a time, then wet the frizz, patted, and combed. Eventually her efforts were rewarded with a head of hair that was once again manageable enough to plait.

Criss-cross, over under, the tamed hair was under full control in an intricate braid, falling to the small of her back, and Mel felt more capable. She bent over the water, scooping a handful of cool water, and splashed her face. Reaching down for one more, she froze with fright. In the rippling water she saw the outline of herself, as well as a man looming above. Without any time to react, a large, dirty hand slammed over her mouth, and the other grabbed tightly around her waist. "Gotcha," a deep voice growled from behind. Mel tried to scream, but the filthy hand was large enough to cover half of her face, and she couldn't suck enough air in or out. The thick arm pulled her slight body closer to his very large, muscular frame and closed in crushingly tight.

Mel swung her elbow back as hard as she could, but the man stepped back expectantly. The fast move saved his abdominals from the quick, sharp jab, but it also moved his thick hands from her lips, leaving her mouth momentarily free. Taking advantage, Mel let out a loud, high-pitched scream that was abruptly cut short. "Thought you could get away again, didn't yeah? Not this time, princess."

It's the man I fought yesterday, she thought, recognizing the deep, sour voice and same acrid smell. Desperately, she kicked back, but the soldier, built solid as steel, swung her body to the side. "Come on, sweetie. Time to get back to camp. You've been gone long enough."

Bucking like an angry mule and emitting muffled screeches, Mel resisted as he dragged her forward. Her mind bounced in a million directions, muddled with anger, confusion, and terror. But the only clear thought that broke through the panic was, *Ransom won't know where I am*. Scrambling, her hand was barely able to slide into her own trouser pocket. Fingers grasped quickly, wrapping around an object, and she hurled it into the grass just before being whisked into the thick brush beyond.

✳ ✳ ✳

With the camp all cleaned and cleared, ashes scattered, and rocks set back in their places, Ransom drew figures in the dirt, waiting. "Oak, elm, oak, scotch, scotch, elm . . ." After naming all the surrounding trees, he paced back and forth, lay in the grass, and rechecked the contents of the bag. Still there was no sign of Mel. Valk, perched on a limb, eyed her person with confusion.

"Do ladies always take this long?" Ransom posed the question to his feathered friend, but his thoughts began to ebb toward worry. *Should I go after her, or is that intruding? Maybe she got lost. Did she leave? No, I have her necklace. Even if she had no loyalty to me, she would never leave that necklace. It's the only thing she has of any value.*

"I'll wait a little longer," he concluded, as if the bird had been in on the entire conversation. "Why don't you check on her instead, would ya?" The falcon cocked its head in response, then straightened. In a quick stroke, she pushed off the bough, sending leaves tumbling down. Veering slightly, the bird of prey soared in Mel's direction, quickly disappearing over the trees.

The longer Ransom waited, the more restless he became. At least he could count on his feathered friend to let him know what was going on. It only took a few minutes, but the bird reappeared in haste, the silhouette of her slick body and wings showing dark against the bright blue sky. As soon as she was in sight, her high-pitched warning reached Ransom's ears. *Someone unknown is near.* Before he could react, a shattering scream sliced through the air, coming from the direction of the stream. Instantly, Ransom heaved the bags over his shoulder, running toward the sound that was unnervingly cut short.

Racing through the endless branches and suffocating limbs, he finally reached the little stream. "Mel? Mel!" he called, though the only answer was the babble of the stream. Turning, searching, completely bewildered, his eyes rested on the ground and the marks left behind. It was obvious a struggle had taken place here, but then the marks elongated, stretching out like something was being dragged. He followed the scuffs as the trees closed in. Only a few steps were obvious before the prints faded, weeds popping up thicker.

Ready to follow blindly, something caught Ransom's eye, half covered in leaves where the brush grew thick again. Running to the object that was clearly out of place, he recognized the thin linen cloth. Quickly, Ransom snatched the tiny package, unwrapped the orb, and hoped that it worked the way he thought it did. As Ransom took a step forward into the thicket, in the direction where the last scraping steps disappeared, the star inside glowed a tiny, almost imperceptible light. Confident now, Ransom plowed forward, pushing through the thick greenery, following the light.

15

THE LAST GIRL

Mel squirmed against a large, aged tree, uncomfortably and completely restrained. Thick rope felt heavy and unreasonably wound around both her and the trunk several times more than necessary. *Apparently they don't trust me*, she thought to herself with a little spite. She'd love to just slide her trusty knife from its hiding place in her boot and slice her way to freedom, but with arms pinned to her sides and rope digging mercilessly into her skin, the sharp little dagger stayed undetected and useless.

The low hum of two Lôurian guards buzzed in the air, heads bowed together in discussion at a small distance from their captive. The big, thick one nodded as the slimmer man spoke. "We'll keep riding west. There's a small tavern south of Stillemäch that we're supposed arrive at in two days' time. We could easily get there by midday on the morrow, but first we should teach this princess a lesson in obedience." He spoke deliberately, turning to sneer at their captive. Black stubble covered the man's jawline, making him look unkempt, but the hair on his head was slicked back and tied into a thong, adding a bit of control to the mix.

"Boss's orders: No harming any girls," the big guy replied simply.

Slick pulled out his own knife, a large, deadly piece, and flipped it forward, catching the blade by the tip and then by the handle. "I don't want to harm her, although she deserves everything she gets. She'd be great for target practice, though!" A slight flick of his strong wrist, and the knife flew through the air, landing just a couple inches above Mel's head. The two erupted in guttural laughter and turned back to their conversation.

Mel sat still, unwilling to flinch, but as soon as their backs were turned, the tension released from her shoulders and she looked around frantically, desperate to find a way out. Legs pulled in toward her body, but with arms tied to the tree the dagger would never be reached. Mel attempted to bend forward, biting at the cord, then wiggled helplessly back and forth.

"I wouldn't do that if I were you," a strong, elder voice stated casually from behind. The man sauntered around the trunk and turned to face the frightened girl. Dull gray hair was pulled back, similar to the other man's, but his face was clean shaven, possessing an air of decorum the other two lacked. "Struggling only pulls the knots tighter when they're done right, and I always do it right. Besides, we have men scattered all around looking for the last girl, which was you. If you happen to escape again, you will never get very far".

Mel stopped her struggle as she registered his words. "Last girl?" she asked simply.

"Yep." He smiled, a little smug. "You girls gave us a nice little run. Some of you never got anywhere, but a couple we had to track."

Boots stepped closer, scuffing in the dirt, and Mel recognized the familiar soft *ting ting* sound that she hoped would never be heard again. Crouching low, invading her space, he surveyed the features before him. With a large, dirty hand, he grabbed a strand of her midnight hair, jostled free from the braid. "You, my lady, gave us a bit of a challenge." The back of his hand barely touched her cheek, sending a chill down her spine. "I can't imagine what a pretty little thing like you did to survive even an hour in the forest, or where you've been hiding." He backed away abruptly. "Now we wait. Once the men return we'll head over to where your lovely sisters await, under lock and key, of course. Then it'll be armed guards and sealed carriage doors until Lôunarike." He laughed, turning away to join his two comrades, leaving Mel alone with her thoughts. She glared at the men, making her face proud and defiant, but the deep brown eyes betrayed her, showing fear.

Overhead, a screech pierced the air from a bird of prey. The sound was nothing out of the ordinary to the others, but Mel's heart instantly beat excitedly. *That has to be Valk, and if it is, then Ransom can't be far behind. Did he find the orb I dropped? Has he really come for me?* She began to wriggle again.

"This would be a lot easier if you quit moving so much," came a voice from behind, muffled by the thick trunk between them.

Immediately, Mel froze, then felt the pressure around her chest suddenly relieve as the thick restraint fell loose, landing in a heap on her lap. Her chest rose as she inhaled a huge, unrestricted breath. Silently, she slid over the slack rope, leaving it lying in a withered heap, and crept around the trunk soundlessly, grateful to be wearing Ransom's old boots instead of the noisy guard's. Making it around the tree, she reached her friend and stopped shoulder-to-shoulder, both backed against the rough, craggy wood. "Thanks," she whispered quickly, eyes curiously darting around, looking for whatever he used to cut the rope. Oddly, there was no blade or tool around. She saw that the rope lying on the ground wasn't just sliced through once, but every layer that wound around her body had been severed. "How did you cut me loose?" she hissed, unable to ascertain the information with her eyes.

"What?" He glanced down at the limp layers of rope. "I just pulled it apart. No big deal. Shh." Distractedly, Ransom peered around the trunk, calculating. As he did so, the thinner guard noticed the absence of their charge.

"She's gone!" Slick yelled, and every person was immediately propelled into motion. The three guards stood, rushing forward while Ransom and Mel pushed off at full speed into the thick undergrowth of the woods. Shouts sputtered in angry spurts from behind as the two fugitives pushed forward, running as fast as they could manage, blazing a trail through the wild brushwood. Hidden in a blanket of leaves, a short jagged branch caught Mel's sleeve with its sharp edges, snagging the material, barely missing skin as she drove forward. Ransom followed behind, nearly falling twice as the shrubbery, compressed so close together, reached out green tendrils and grabbed at his feet. Gradually, the area changed and the entangling leaves and limbs began to space apart, becoming easier to maneuver. Ransom stopped abruptly. "I'll fight them off. You keep going," he commanded, his wide chest rising heavily with each labored breath.

Mel skidded to a halt, whipping around. "No! You can't fight all three guards on your own. That's suicide!" It wasn't meant as an insult, but more of genuine concern. She'd grown fond of this boy, the first person she had ever truly been herself with, and she wasn't not ready to say goodbye.

"Trust me," he said quickly. "I'm stronger than I look, remember? Now go!"

Swept up in a current of emotion, Mel hurried back to her friend, popped up onto the tips of her toes, and gave him a small, meaningful kiss. In that moment she didn't question if he liked her, she wasn't wondering if he approved of a kiss, and she had no feeling of embarrassment. This was the second time he had offered up his life to save her own, and she gave him the only thing she had to gave in return—her heart. "Stay safe," was all she could think to say before sprinting away like a spooked doe. As the branches bent and whipped to her movements, she only thought of one thing: *I hope that won't be our last and only kiss.*

Racing as fast as her legs could move, she burst through the trees into an opening. Still running, she soon saw why the trees had stopped growing, coming to a halt at the edge of a deep, jagged ravine. Her head whipped side to side, searching the thick cut in the earth's surface spreading as far as she could see on either side. The walls of the crack sloped at a slight angle, descending, rough and steep. Patches of stubborn weeds and boulders scattered all along the decline, with dirt or smaller rock filling in the gaps. The other side wouldn't be too far away if she had a bridge of some sort, but as it was, it was much too far for her to jump. *If only Ransom were here with me. He'd know what to do.* Mel stopped suddenly, finally able to think clearly, and the chaos calmed into reason. "What am I thinking? He can't fight those awful men. If I leave him, he'll die." Mel turned back the way she came. *I may not be able to help much, but I'm not going to leave him alone.* Making up her mind, the brave maiden doubled back into the trees, hoping it wasn't too late.

16

BRUISED AND BROKEN

Standing alone in the clearing, his heart thumped loudly in his chest. The guards were catching up quickly, and the young man had very little time to prepare. *Three against one.* He had thought about this type of scenario before when obsessively training alone in his tower, but this was the first time he'd be putting his knowledge to practical use. Surveying the area quickly, he spotted large stones about the size of his head. *Three stones for three men. That will do.*

In no time the guards burst through the forestry, sweat soaked, furious, and thirsty for blood. The two younger men approached with swords already drawn, their thick forearms unfazed by the weight of the heavy steel. The older man gave a signal to halt, stopping the men from advancing, then called out toward their unknown opponent. "Where is she?"

"Who?" Ransom answered with a confident smile, though his heart raced faster than ever.

"Let's just kill him and keep going," growled the thinner of the two young soldiers. "We can't afford to lose her again." The remark was pointed directly at the larger man, who glared back with disdain.

"Not my fault the brat wiggled out of my arms like a fish. Besides, I'm the one that found her again, aren't I?" the big guy shot back at his companion.

The older man never took his eyes off of Ransom. "We don't want to kill you, but we will. Now where is she?"

"I may be young, but I'm strong. Are you sure you want to risk it?" Ransom answered, sounding more confident than he felt.

"All right boys. She's definitely a runner and we're losing distance. Kill this boy so we can get going," the older man commanded, lowering his arm in signal.

With the orders finally given, the two happily advanced with swords glinting in the sunlight. Boots tromped over grasses and ferns, making a tiny jingling noise with each step. "You chose the wrong day to be a hero, boy," the slick younger guard taunted with pleasure.

Without waiting to find out if these men knew how to use their steel, Ransom squatted low, grabbed one of the small boulders with his gloved hands, and lifted it with ease. The quick move of their target surprised the two, causing a moment of hesitation as they chanced a sideways glance between each other. The big guy shrugged toward the other as if to say, *What could he possibly do with that?* Taking the cue, Slick turned back to their opponent with a sneer. "You're dead, and that girl is ours. Don't worry, we'll take good care of her, but first I'll break her legs." Then they advanced with force.

The words of the soldier lit a raging fire deep in Ransom's soul, and he shifted the small boulder to one hand, cocking back his arm, his eyes narrowed with deadly focus. Taking a step not unlike a Greek Olympian hurling the shot put, he launched the small boulder straight at the sneering face. Flying with incredible speed, the rock hit its target with a sickening crunch, smashing Slick hard in the temple. Instantly the injured man fell, knocked unconscious. The larger man froze in his tracks, shocked. No man should be able to throw a stone of that size farther than a few rods' length, let alone with that much speed. Still, shock only lasted a fleeting moment, and then, trained as he was, the surprise dissipated quickly as the thick soldier advanced again.

Without hesitation, Ransom crouched, pulling up a second boulder. Only taking a second to aim, he threw with all his might. Trained in combat, the thick mountain of a man predicted Ransom's moves and ducked to avoid a blow to the head, but Ransom wasn't aiming high this time. The stone tore through the air, striking flesh and bone as the solid boulder smashed straight into the man's knee. Instantly he fell, with howls of pain erupting into the air.

Two down, one to go. Ransom glanced up, but the third was nowhere to be seen. A warning screeched from above, letting him know that something was behind. Whipping around quickly, he caught a flash of gray and black as the seasoned guard attacked from behind. The soldier lunged forward with his sword, and Ransom sidestepped just in time to witness the steel blade pierce the air where his back had been. The swordsman followed through, unable to interrupt the force of his trajectory, and Ransom took advantage of the forward motion by swinging his fist straight into the man's midsection. "Oof!" The guard let out a heaving sound as wind was completely knocked from his core. He started to fall, mouth gaping as he struggled for breath. Another swing, this time to the jaw, forced the soldier to the ground in a miserable heap.

Swiping the sword from the incapacitated man, Ransom surveyed quickly, satisfied with his work, and turned to bolt. Leaves rustled from straight ahead, signaling that someone else was approaching quickly, and he pointed the newly acquired blade forward, holding steel at the ready. He raised the hilt, poised to charge, as the person burst through the trees, springing forward with her dagger in hand. Ransom lunged but instantly lowered the blade at the sight of her reappearance. "What are you doing here?" he yelled, a little too forcefully.

"I came to help. Three soldiers against one man doesn't seem very fair." Mel scanned the area, noting the guards on the ground. "Or is it too fair? What on earth happened here?"

"No time. Let's go," he called back in haste. Holding the sword to the side, he grabbed her hand and pulled, crashing into the forest.

"Ransom!" she yelled, trying to keep up. The warning fell short as her breath failed. "We can't . . . There's no way . . . " They burst through the edge of the trees, running at full speed, and Mel slowed down, trying to pull back. Caught short, Ransom jerked backward and turned to see what was creating the problem. Mel stood doubled over, trying to catch her breath. "Ravine." She could barely get out through gasps. "Too big. Can't jump."

Ransom whipped his head around, finally noticing the jagged lip, and scanned the edge of the forest, looking side to side. Just outside the clearing, an enormous log lay nestled in the grass from a large, recently fallen tree. "Timber," was all he said, jogging to the horizontal hunk of wood.

Confused, Mel followed slowly from behind. "What do you plan on doing with that?" she asked, unable to keep the tone of her voice level.

"We could use it as a bridge," he answered pointedly, as if it was obvious to anyone with two eyes, then started mumbling more to himself. "It looks like it'll be long enough, and thick too. Yep, it'll support us just fine. Watch out, would ya?"

"Watch out? I don't think the two of us are going to get that massive thing very far. What are you going to do? Move a whole tree by yourself?" Mel spit out with a mix of disbelief and panic.

The young man gave her his slight half-smile. "That's exactly what I'm going to do. Here, hold this, would ya?" He handed off the sword and bags, then walked to the center of the trunk, squatted down, and, after sliding his arms under the enormously solid log, began to lift slowly. At first, the tree was reluctant to budge, having settled in nicely among the wild greenery and blooms, but little by little Ransom lifted. Chips of bark, chunks of moss, and even a few mushrooms fell away as the massive trunk released hold from its resting place.

Mel stepped back, her big eyes becoming even bigger. She opened her mouth to speak, but no sound came out. Ransom hoisted the log onto his shoulder and turned back to the ravine. Quickly and confidently, he shuffled forward, chest out and face calm. Reaching the jagged edge, he lowered one end to the ground while large hands firmly gripped the sides, forcing the enormous log to stand tall as it had for centuries before. Carefully, he lowered the heavy giant to the ground, anchoring his side until the log once again lay parallel to the ground. Panting slightly, half-smile clearly showing pride, he turned to Mel. "After you."

"What just happened?" Mel mumbled, rooted to her spot, completely stunned.

Shouts from behind snapped Mel from shock to panic. Hearing Valk's screech above, Ransom glanced over Mel's head, toward the trees behind. "I'll explain later. Let's go now!" The easygoing boy disappeared as the man in charge took over. Mel saw the transformation and immediately responded by climbing onto the log, as fast as she could safely move. Heart racing, pounding in her chest, only one thought repeated in her mind. *Don't get caught. Don't fall. Don't get caught. Don't fall.* Brown eyes never looked back, but her body felt the slight jerk as her partner boarded the trunk behind, sending soft vibrations with every step.

Men crashed through the thick wall of trees, shouting loudly as they pummeled forward. The older guard charged ahead, accompanied by Slick with half his face covered in swelling purple bruises. Pain did little to slow a man fueled by hate and adrenaline. Behind, two more men burst through the roughage. *Some of the searching guards must have found their beaten compeers.* Immediately, they spotted their target crossing the makeshift bridge and the elder shouted commands, all sprinting in their direction.

Mel reached the other side of the ravine and jumped off the trunk as soon as she was able, landing on her feet lightly. Relieving her arms, she pressed the heavy sword, tip down, into the soft earth, then whipped around to see Ransom only a few feet behind. The guards were approaching way too quickly, and it wouldn't be long until they were on the log as well. "Hurry!" she shouted, worried they wouldn't have enough time to distance themselves and hide. "They're almost here!"

Ransom stepped the last foot and dropped down on the other side of the trunk, making a split-second decision. With all his might, he kicked the huge log, just as the first Lōurian boot rested on top. Flying sideways into the deep ravine, the tree descended quickly, throwing the guard onto his back in a cloud of dirt. Within no time, the heavy wooden bridge hit the bottom with a startlingly loud crash as the timber cracked and splintered. Ransom turned to share a victorious smile, but no one was there. Instead, a scream echoed from below.

At the same moment the log was kicked to the side, a broken branch caught the strap around Mel's shoulder, violently pulling the girl over the edge without care. Tumbling down the wall, head over heels, she rolled onto her stomach and dug her hands into the patches of dirt, desperately seeking for an anchor, using anything her fingers could wrap around. Grasping handfuls of hearty weeds, she was able to slow her descent, but only for a moment as the weak plants released their grip in the soil too easily. Sharp, eroded edges jutted from the slope, banging against her entire body, but none of the blows compared to the sudden explosion that resonated from her elbow. Lightning struck her arm as the bone crashed down on a small boulder, and she was lucid enough to know that it was broken. Another scream tried to form in her throat, this time from pain more than fear, but the constant tumbling and dirt flying in her face prevented the sound from escaping. Finally, after what seemed like an eternity, she landed heavily on the rocky ground below.

The whole thing happened in a matter of seconds, and all Ransom could do was stand frozen, helpless as Mel struggled for her life. The guards remained just as still, unsure and entranced. As the dusty, beaten body fell to the earth, they began to pull out of the spell, looking to each other, waiting for a command. Ransom watched the men tensely, trying to decipher their cues, waiting for them to make a move. He stood on the edge over her unconscious body, willing to do whatever it took to protect Mel from the scavengers that preyed on the helpless. *I will never let you have her.*

Back and forth the men debated, looking down, then across the gap at the young stranger standing as sentry. Ransom bent low, picking up a rock at his feet, and held it tightly, nearly crushing the stone to dust. He poised, ready to throw again. Slowly, however, the threat was eased as the angry men accepted the lot before them. No one wanted a dead woman. Three turned to go, but the fourth, the older man, stood his ground a moment longer, staring across the empty space. The gray man studied his opponent intensely. Ransom felt the loathing from the man's countenance, and sent it back with interest. In the next moment, the guard gave a small, distinct bow of respect and acceptance. "She's all yours," he pronounced loudly, turning on his heels and heading back the way the others had retreated.

Ransom stayed strong, standing on the edge as the last man sank into the folds of greenery. Finally, with all traces of the guards gone, his shoulders dropped as his eyes darted, searching for a way down. There, nearly invisible, a thin deer trail zigzagged to the bottom. Quickly, he picked his way down as fast as he could while maintaining balance and footing on the dangerous wall.

Boots hit the canyon floor, instantly sprinting over loose rocks as he catapulted himself to her side. The beauty lay face down, and Ransom skidded to a halt, landing on his knees, unaware of any pain. "Mel!" he shouted, a little louder than expected. "Mel," he tried again, reining in the panic. "Don't be dead. Please. I can't help you if you're dead." Resting his shaking hands on her sides, he turned her over gently. Ugly gray bruising spread quickly over half her forehead, and angry scratches slashed across her beautiful face. Delicate hands now showed broken, dirt-filled nails, while cuts beginning on her fingers sliced up the arms, showing red through the jagged holes in her shirt. One arm in particular lay at an odd angle, and Ransom realized it was busted.

Filthy and covered in dust, her trousers had a few minor tears and a few small snags. One boot was scuffed and scratched, while the other had gone missing. "Oh, Mel, I'm so sorry," he said softly, brushing the dark hair from her eyes. With no more words, he cradled her in his arms, leaning forward to rest his forehead on hers, carefully avoiding the bruise. Slightly, almost imperceptibly, he heard the small exhale of a shallow breath and lifted his head in surprise, sure that she had been lost forever. "Mel!" he exclaimed with relief and joy. "You're alive! I thought you left me."

Imelda's eyes twitched under closed, swollen lids in reaction to his voice, but otherwise she made no move to wake.

"I got this. Don't worry. You'll be good as new in no time."

Slowly, her lungs began to rise and fall in deeper rounds as she hung on to life with every ounce of her fading strength. Ransom choked back dismay, becoming that man-in-charge once more. "Imelda," he whispered in her ears,

"I can help you. Trust me." There was no indication that she understood, but he didn't expect any reaction. Lifting her wrist, so small in his big hands, he placed the scraped palm on his own shoulder. He held the hand still and spoke as if to a conscious companion. "Now just stay there. I'm going to recite something. Don't let go." Ransom cleared his throat. "Strengthen marrow, strengthen bones. Time reversed, stand all alone. Recover, revive, redeem, renew. Become the person that I once knew."

Immediately a surge spread throughout her body, starting at the tips of her fingers that lay limp on his shoulder, rushing down to her chest, and spreading like wildfire to the top of her head and the tips of her toes. Her eyes opened wide, vividly aware. Her breath deepened, inhaling easily, while the pain in her head and muscles subsided. Wounds faded until they vanished completely. Lightning receded, inch by inch, from the broken limb, and the bone moved into place on its own accord until the joint snapped back together, whole again.

The entire life-altering experience was over in a flash, and in the wake was left a baffled, perfectly whole Imelda. She stared up at Ransom in shock, with the lovely rose coloring back in her cheeks. Her lips opened to speak, but her eyes asked more than she could convey in words.

"Come on," Ransom said. "Let's get out of here. Don't ask. Once we're safe, I think I need to explain a couple things. You think you can walk?"

Instinctively, she shook her head no but realized that it didn't hurt to do so, and carefully attempted to rise. Standing with surprising ease, Mel felt both rested and invigorated. She opened her left arm a few times in disbelief and patted her body down. Everything was in perfect condition, some parts even better than before. "You have a lot of explaining to do," she remarked through a dry throat, eyeing him suspiciously.

"I know, but let's get out of here first. Here, take my hand and I'll help you climb up." He reached for her hand.

Mel smiled slyly. "With the way I feel right now, you might want to take mine."

17

CHEMISTRY

"Careful. Watch your step here. This part is steep." Ransom's concerned comments were welcome as Mel picked her way back up the deer trail. He held her hand protectively until he was finally able to pull her over the lip. Back on solid ground, he turned, stoic and rigid, scanning their surroundings for any sign of the soldiers.

"I'm dead, remember? No one is looking for me anymore."

"You don't know that for sure. They could still be waiting anywhere," he said, focused on the area where they had disappeared.

"They're not," Mel replied firmly. She felt the tension and lay a hand gently on his back. His muscles relaxed in response. Slowly, she walked around to face him. "I guess I should thank you for pushing me. It wasn't fun, but at least I'm free." She smiled slyly and gave a small wink, then turned to the forest. "Just in case, though, let's get going." The two entered into the cover of the trees quickly, continuing west toward Stillemäch.

"I don't think we'll make it to the city before nightfall like we planned." Mel talked over her shoulder, leading the way. "What do you think about roughing it one more night?"

Another night alone with you sounds perfect, he thought as he watched the newly plaited hair dance with each step in front of him. *How about seven more nights?* He'd become quite fond of the rebellious lady, and for good reason. She was quick witted when her guard was down, feisty, and fair. Inexperienced as she was in the simple things, he could see in her eyes the knowledge, hurt, and complexity that was once her life. She was a rare jewel that upon first glance was beautiful, but once placed to the eye, multi-dimensional facets revealed themselves. Some were perfect and some were imperfect, but that's what made the stone so rare. Instead of voicing his thoughts, however, he replied with a simple, "I'm okay with it if you are."

"All right then, we'll look for a place to camp in a bit." With that the two march forward, distancing themselves from the ravine and the guards as much as possible. Silence fell over the pair as they walked soberly, each left to their own consuming thoughts—one trying to decide the best way to ask, while the other tried to find an explanation. A little past midday, they stumbled onto a small, secluded knoll scattered with rich green clover and tiny flowers, shaded from the blaring sun. "Gorgeous," Mel gasped, bending down to feel the soft, welcoming blooms.

Ransom smiled, swinging the satchel from his shoulder. "Seems like a good spot to take a break. Wha'dya say?"

"Sounds good to me," the maiden replied, settling in the soft, flowing ground cover. They retrieved leftover ginger biscuits and jerky from the sack, and Mel passed a tangy morsel to her companion, then bit into her own. *Still as good as the first day.* "Wow, Nedgie has a gift."

"Mmm hmm," Ransom responded, swallowing a swig of the beet juice.

They ate in silence, allowing the life to bravely hum all around. The subtle brushing of leaves dancing in the breeze created a soft background for the chatter of the invisible birds above. Not far off, a critter dug through the soft underbrush of the forest floor, hidden from sight but clearly present and determined. A pair of daring squirrels ventured forth to the dangerous ground, snatching a few acorns before hauling their loot back, far up the wide trunk of a great gnarled elm. The tiny scratching of their paws was irregular, playful, and incredibly quick. Even Valk participated in the wooded symphony, screeching once, then twice, before resting soundless on a branch above her person.

Mel settled back on her arms, focusing on the busy squirrels with fascination until their bushy tails disappeared into their hollow. "How old do you suppose that tree is?" she asked dreamily.

The young man followed her gaze, blue eyes landing on the squirrel's lair. "The width of the trunk suggests about one-hundred fifty, give or take fifteen years." Mel responded with a curious stare, and Ransom shrugged. "I've read several books on trees and plants in general," he added as an explanation.

"Hmm." She smiled, then turned her focus back to the old soul. "What do you think it would be like to live that long?"

"The things you would see, people you'd meet, places you'd go. I'm sure the stories would be fascinating," he imagines thoughtfully. "I'll tell ya what it's like when I get there."

She laughed softly, then turned to see his face, gentle but serious. "What do you mean 'when you get there'? Does this have something to do with what happened in the ravine?"

Ransom faced Mel, trying to find the best way to begin. "I don't know everything about my abilities, but this much I'm certain: I'll never mature past my prime, and I'll live forever that way. It's a power that I have had my whole life. Some kind of gift of strength," he started, turning away to look down at tiny pink petals. "I'm stronger than a normal man, but I'm not really sure how strong. I've never been able to test it out properly, but Father referred to it as the 'strength of a mountain' once, whatever that means." She sat silently, absorbing the details, so he continued. "I have strength, but I can also restore strength to others."

Mel studied his face as she asked, "Is that what you did for me? Restored my strength?"

"Yes, in a way. It helped that you were already youthful. It made everything work even quicker than usual. When I gave you your strength back, your body healed itself instantly. Better, even." He smiled proudly.

"What was wrong with my body before?" Mel snapped, more playful than defensive.

"Nothing," he answered quickly. "You were—I mean are—perfect. Wait, that's not what I meant. But I did." Stopping himself, Ransom simply sighed when he saw the humor in Mel's eyes. Exasperated, the struggling man pleaded, "Could you just give me a little break? I'm still getting used to talking to people, and not just birds." They both chuckled lightheartedly, and he lifted his hands to look at the leather gloves, becoming sober once more. *Tell her everything. No more secrets.* "That's why I wear these. Believe it or not, I don't wear gloves as a fashion choice. It's for protection. If I get a deep enough cut anywhere on my hands, I could lose my gift forever."

Mel studied the leather sitting snuggly around large hands as he turned them over in concentration. "That makes sense."

He stopped studying the gloves and returned his attention to the dark beauty. No judgment, greed, or adversity showed in those deep brown eyes like he had been conditioned and prepared to see. Instead, she looked at him with interest and compassion. "Is that the reason you've been living in that awful tower?"

Blue eyes fell to his feet, and for the first time the mask of confidence dropped as well, leaving complete vulnerability, "Yeah. Like I said, over-protective father. He's worried that people will want to capture me, maybe lock me up, possibly even kill me. People are cold-blooded, brutal, and selfish by nature. That's what he told me. So I was raised in a place no one could ever find me, to keep me from all the evil."

Mel reached out, gently placing a hand on Ransom's shoulder. "People can be terrible, but there's more to this world than human flaws. There's a balance, really. In everything you'll always find a balance. Take me, for example." His head turned to the side in surprise, not once having thought to compare his own circumstance with hers. With a small smile, she continued, "I've been held in a castle all my life as well. Sure I was free to go outside, and I had other ladies to talk with, but I was never allowed to live the way I wanted, or choose anything for myself."

"I can relate," Ransom remarked empathetically, understanding the new, deepening bond between them.

"The difference," Mel continued, "is that you were kept hidden for your exceptional attributes, and I was sold for mine."

"So Father was right all along. The world is too cruel for people who are different," Ransom stated, shoulders slumping with defeat.

A soft hand glided down his shoulder, following the tight muscles of his bicep, over the forearm, and grabbed hold of his large, leather-clad hand. He looked back at her with surprise, having never held someone's hand before, let alone the dainty one of a woman. At first his own fingers stiffened involuntarily, but soon relaxed into a natural sort of way, melding the two into one like well-worked clay. She scooted closer so that there was only a sliver of space between their bodies, her other hand crossing over to grab a hold of his arm. Lowering her head to the side, she rested against his shoulder and sighed. "There are so many rotten, ugly, and evil things in this world. I pretty much gave up on humanity and goodness when I was forced to leave my home, but you've opened my eyes to stuff I hadn't noticed before. The goodness of simple things. This world is beautiful, even the tiny insignificant twigs and mice." His sandy head leaned lightly against her ebony hair as he listened. "And people. People can be awful if they choose to be, but maybe we meet the wrong people or experience hard things so we can appreciate the right people when they come crashing into our lives."

Ransom glanced to the side, catching a glimpse of the top of Mel's head, and silently admired how beautiful her raven hair looked plaited. Incredibly, her black locks seemed to capture the scents of the forest as she passed through, and irresistibly smelled like a combination of clay, fresh rosemary, and pine. Allowing the silence to linger for several heartbeats, he closed his eyes, enjoying the scents and closeness. "So, am I the 'right' kind of people then?" Ransom asked, with a sly half-smile, breaking the moment.

Pulling herself straight, she looked at him intensely, then, in a flash, pushed herself forward, laying full lips gently on his smirking mouth. In the next instant, the soft, desirable lips pulled away. Releasing his hand from the sweet hold, she patted his leg twice. "You're all right, I guess," she said playfully, pushing herself to stand, "but I didn't feel any magical power come from those lips!"

Ransom protested, "That's not fair. I wasn't ready. I'll show you power, if that's what you're looking for!"

"Easy there." Mel smiled, picking up her satchel while backing away coolly. "We have a long walk ahead of us still, and lots of information to digest."

He swiped his own bag and trailed after her. "Well, how was that fair? You attack me while I'm unaware, then insult my stunned efforts," he reasoned as they continued their journey

"You want me to teach you about the niceties of high-born life, correct?" Mel asked, flipping her long dark braid while walking ahead, a little victory in her step.

"Correct," Ransom replied, matter-of-factly.

Mel stopped, turned back to Ransom, and closed the gap until they were face to face, her looking up and him down, inches apart. Time stood still for a moment as Ransom looked into Mel's big beautiful eyes, smelled her hair once more, and felt her breath. "A lady must take advantage when the gentleman is most vulnerable, but never reveal all her tricks at once, or the interest would vanish in thin air. It's called flirting. Something they don't teach a person living in a tower, I bet. You'll learn quickly, though.

It comes rather naturally to some." She swung her leg around, body following smoothly, and began walking forward again with a little sway to her hips.

Hmm, flirting. That was never mentioned in the countless textbooks he had read in his life. Biology, anatomy, physiology—none ever mentioned the elusive idea of playful banter, delicate calculations of when to hold a hand, or the correct measure of a moment in which a kiss was appropriate. He had never been a fan of being tricked, but this seemed like a game he'd be happy to win, or lose.

18

A SOLDIER'S TALE

As the sun gradually set, trees, flowers, and even creatures all surrendered their boldness and bright hues in exchange for a progressively darkening muted gray, slowly losing their individuality, blending together into one. Draven paced himself on familiar trails, slower than when he first started that morning, but making good time by choosing the paths that headed straight east through the vast forest, with no respite and no veering from the course. Irritated, his mule followed, becoming increasingly stubborn with the lack of food and rest. "You'll get your break when I get my flower back," he mumbled to the mule, pulling forward on the reigns.

Deeper than anger, Draven was filled with terror that chilled him to his weakening bones. Losing his golden goose, the one precious possession that had kept him youthful and strong all these years, meant rapid aging, ending only in death. *This will not be my end.* Weakening as he was, his feet continued stubbornly onward, and the steady pace finally paid off as the small party emerged from the forest, stepping onto a worn highway curving through the woods, connecting north to south. A small distance up the old, windy road candlelight spilled from the small windows of a shabby highway tavern.

"Finally," he muttered to his equine companion, "a place with secrets for sale." Draven pulled the reins again, walking toward the dilapidated roadhouse, thinking through all the scenarios in his mind before they happened. *The best situation I could hope for is that Ransom is inside that filthy place right now, drinking with his new Lōurian friend, feeling reckless and free, and easy to manipulate. The second best option is that the boy has been here already and has left going south. It's not ideal, but at least I will know I'm on the right track.*

Black, dusty boots scuffed against the packed dirt, and his exhausted feet failed him, tripping over themselves. Reins slipped from his grip as the aging man fell forward, chin scraping hard on the rough earth. Groaning, he rolled onto his side in the grass lining the highway. Though his face ached, it wasn't the only part that hurt. Muscles screamed with knots and strain. Flesh on the palms of his weakening hands gaped open with fresh wounds as the skin noticeably thinned with each hour. Shaking his head slowly, Draven pushed himself to sit. The fall created an interruption, and he used the recess to assess the damage, feeling a small, wet sensation roll down his jawline and drip on his chest.

Reaching up, he felt the coolness of blood, and his brow furrowed as he attempted to recall the last time he had bled. It had been years since he'd been hurt at all. A perk of the healing powers was quick thought and reaction. With the magical strength in his bones, it felt as though he could see the tiniest pin from miles away, and with that kind of forethought one almost entirely avoided accidents and injuries. The loss of acute vision and quickness of mind was infuriating.

Draven sat still for only a moment longer, catching his breath and bracing himself for the taxing work ahead. Even the simple act of pulling oneself to stand was a chore now. Anger began to creep up once more, and like a tidal wave, it pulled back, seemingly harmless. Then the next instant built with momentum and crashed with fury, all consuming. *How could that boy be so selfish? So reckless? So inconsiderate!* The aging hunter saw red as deep as the blood on his chin, and with the force of rage, he hurled himself up and forward. "That boy will pay."

Little by little, Draven made his way up the road, finally approaching the tiny tavern. The high-pitched squeak of rusted metal pierced the silence as the sign hanging from the eaves swayed back and forth ever so slightly on its hinges. *The Amber Horn* was painted on the wooden sign under the large skull of a big-horned ram in proud display for travelers to see. Outside the shabby rest stop sat a two carriage caravan, waiting patiently for whomever was inside. Horses stood still and calm in the dimming eve, content with a welcomed break from travel, and Draven took note of the strong black stallions standing tall even at ease. They shifted slightly on thick hooves as the newcomer approached with a lone mule in tow, but not a sound escaped, nor a hair swayed. Manes were gathered in rows of knots, as well as tails, in the Lōurian signature style, creating a very tight and pristine-looking team.

His eyes followed the harness that held the first group of powerful creatures, letting his gaze glide over the carriage hitched behind. On the 'small door, painted in Lōurian flourish, was the same seal as was found on the guard's clothing back at the tower. *There must be some connection. Is the man with Ransom a rogue guard from this group, perhaps? A deserter who abandoned his post, now running from the law?* Another suspicion drew in the withering man. *Perhaps King Barrett decided to reinstate the search for his firstborn, hiring soldiers from the neighboring kingdom to keep things quiet.* If that was the case, the soldier could have finally found what the entire kingdom had sought for nearly twenty years.

Whatever the case, speculation wouldn't help Draven now, and he dismissed his convoluted scenarios before they forged a new sense of panic. Then, his eyes rested on the handle of the carriage door, or rather, above. *A padlock, secured to keep thieves out, or is it there to keep someone in?* The carriage rocked slightly, and a dark silhouette passed by the window. Completely obscured by the filmy glass, grime and darkening light, it was enough for Draven to know that whoever was imprisoned inside was female. He turned away without any more thought for the contents inside and proceeded to the thick door. As he approached, the scent of drink and unwashed men hit his nostrils. *Soldiers must be inside.*

Pushing the door, Draven stepped into the thick acrid musk of men in close quarters mingled with notes of yeast and overripe fruit. Scanning the small, dirty room quickly, his shoulders released their tension. The predicted soldiers took up most of the space, but there was no sign of his target in sight. *He's not here. What a relief, and what a disappointment. Should I keep moving, or stay for a meal?* He shrugged. *A meal won't hurt,* he thought, and slid in inconspicuously. Slowly, aching and worn, he walked along the wall and pulled up a chair in the corner, dragging the wooden legs on the warped planks of the worn floor. Even with the unintentional sound, no one cared to glance his way.

Seething, the Lōurian men sat in the center of the room, split between two round tables, some worse for wear than others. Scowls and low grumblings sibilated as the men brooded, drawing Draven's attention. Two nursed wounds quietly, obviously in pain, while a third, an older man with ashen hair, recounted their troubles, all the while nursing an injured jaw. Apparently, the men had been sent to retrieve a maiden that had escaped their grasp. "We found the last wench," he pronounced, meeting hearty cheers in response. The tale went on. "Tied to a tree, waiting for the rest . . ." The details bore Draven, and his mind wandered. The seasoned guard stood, raised with the excitement of the tale. "A man came out of nowhere and stole her away. We gave chase, and squared off with the thief."

Uninterested, Draven lifted his arm to grab the attention of the barkeep but stopped.

"Strength like I've never seen. The lad threw a boulder at Khal's head, knocking him unconscious. Grish caught another square in the knee, shattering the bones to pieces."

The younger, thinner guard moaned at the sound of his name. Patting his fellow on the shoulder, the elder paced around a table and lowered himself into a rickety chair, raising a horn in salute to his injured comrades before taking a gulp. Silence fell as the others waited in anticipation. Coming up for air, he continued, "I, myself, tried to take the boy on from behind, but he turned just in time for my blade to pierce the air and his fist met my gut. The blow knocked me to my knees! I have never been hit so hard in my life . . ."

Draven's heart jumped quickly. *I'm on the right track! They saw Ransom. It had to be him.* His mind churned as he attempted to formulate a new plan and predicted the moves of an eighteen-year-old dreamer. *Where could he have gone from here? Ransom had a skirmish with these men, but who was the girl they spoke of? Was she Lôurian? Or . . . had they collected her? Yes, that's it, and others from the looks of the locked carriages outside.*

Finally, a direction. The road offered two options: south to Lôunarike or north to Stillemäch. The game Draven hunted was running from these brutes, not toward them, which eliminated south. Snapping out of his silent deliberations with a plan in place, he pushed the dilapidated chair back to stand when he caught the last of the soldier's tale.

"Dead! The girl fell ten, no, twenty meters down the side of the gorge like a little rag doll. I saw her head smash against a boulder. When she landed"—he paused, shaking the gray head solemnly—"I watched and waited, but she never got up." The hardened warrior seemed almost sorry that they lost her. Sorry that they'd be reprimanded, not so sorry for the loss of the innocent life. Another swig from the horn created suspense, and Draven seized the lull in the story, speaking out before any others could.

"How do you know she was dead?" he called from the back of the room.

Heads whipped around to peer at the intruder daring to insert himself in the midst of this private conversation. "Yeh don't think I know what death looks like?" roared the old guard as he dropped his cup onto the scarred table and raised himself to stand, meeting the level of his challenger. Sizing up the man, Draven concluded that, though the oldest in the bunch, this soldier was not yet past his prime and carried the added benefit of strength and calculation.

Dropping his head as a beta would, Draven adorned the pretense of humility, beginning again. "My apologies, captain. I did not mean to offend. I have no doubt your conclusion was both complete and accurate. I just wondered if the girl was in fact completely dead."

The guard stood with shoulders squared but now released the tension and swiped his horn for another gulp. All waited patiently for his response. Wiping his upper lip, the man eyed the weak traveler with more curiosity than suspicion. "She was dead," he declared firmly, to which Draven nodded with satisfaction and headed for the door. "Or, at least she was all but dead. If she wasn't at the time, she had only minutes to live. The fall was brutal, and no person, especially such a dainty lil thing, could have survived."

This addition stopped Draven in his tracks. There it was. Inconclusive death. *Ransom had been with this girl, and if she hadn't died in the fall, then she was most likely alive and skipping by now. I know the healing that boy possesses firsthand, and I know his heart. He would not hesitate using his power on anyone he cares for. The gallant fool already risked his life to save that mystery girl from being captured. He certainly wouldn't bother concealing his true powers if she had been on the brink of certain death.* With no time to waste, he left the tavern, exiting into the darkness.

Breathing in the clean night air, darkness enveloped the entirety of his surroundings, but the inability to see had no effect on Draven's resolve. His direction was suddenly clear. Stillemäch was where they were headed now, not south. She, Ransom's companion, was running from the Lôurian guards, and Ransom desired to join the royal cavalry. Stillemäch was the perfect compromise for both parties and the absolute worse place Draven could have imagined. Though exhausted and achy, he untied the reins of his old mule and turned north, forcing his feet to step one in front of the other. He would follow this road, carving through the wilds of the forest, until at last he reached the prize once more. Though his pace was slower still than before, Draven found the fleeting strength inside himself and pushed forward.

19

MARIGOLD GIFTS

Lying side by side among the hearty green and yellow blades in the protection of the trees, the two travelers rested comfortably. Though sticks poked and the ground was uneven, neither cared to move, comfort coming from the closeness and intimacy they shared. As morning broke, Ransom was the first to open his eyes. There, wrapped in her own blanket, the beautifully tranquil face of Imelda rested so close their noses almost touched. He couldn't help but stare for a moment, studying the smooth olive skin, long black lashes, full lips barely parting as she continued to slumber. A warmth overpowered Ransom, and he knew any man would count himself lucky to wake to this face every day of their life. Dampening his thoughts, he remembered how far away Smarahav truly was. This sleeping beauty, his friend and companion, would leave today and travel what felt like a world away.

Shaking the thought from his mind, he glanced at the thick black hair, wild from the night, framing her face in harmonious chaos, and he slowly reached to pluck a leaf from her crown. Pulling ever so gently, he managed to free the green adornment without moving one strand of hair. "Maybe I liked that there." Mel spoke softly, eyes remaining closed.

Ransom smiled. "Well, if that's the case, I have a whole forest of leaves just for you." Grabbing a handful, he raised them over her head.

"You wouldn't dare," she challenged sleepily but firm. One rogue leaf escaped his grasp and floated down easily, landing on her rounded cheek. Brown eyes flashed open. "Hey!"

"Oops." Ransom dropped the handful on the ground by his side. "Here, I'll get that." Sweeping his hand lightly, he brushed the incredibly smooth skin, sending the leaf behind her head to land with its fellows below. He rolled down on his back and shivered, finding the spot chilled since he was on his side. Looking up, he slid one hand behind his head, the other close to Mel. "Do you think destinies could change, or are they constant no matter what comes into your life?"

Deep, thought-provoking questions proved difficult to process so soon after waking, but Mel attempted to answer. "I don't really believe in destiny anymore. I was told what my purpose is all my life, and now that I'm free I can't imagine that there is only one path for each person. Why not do it all?" She paused, still curled on her side, studying the strong jawline that shaped Ransom's face. "I don't think you have to choose one thing over the other." She reached over and lay her hand on top of his, wrapping fingers lightly. His response was automatic as he folded the slender fingers into his own. The stillness lasted for only a moment, and then the forest gradually awakened as woodland creatures began their daily chores. Above, morning songs danced in the air with increasing volume, and the joyous energy was infectious. Mel squeezed his hand before releasing it, then sat up, letting her unruly hair fall over her shoulders and down her back. "Speaking of choices, do we have any options for breakfast in that bag, or were we foraging this morning?"

Ransom followed, sitting up as well, slightly chuckling at the wild mess that was Mel's hair. "I'm afraid this morning we search for our breakfast in the brambles."

The frazzled beauty brushed her fingers through tangles self-consciously, pulling back until the mane was contained in a high knot. "Well then, should we get started? I'm starving, and we have a big day ahead."

* * *

Parallel ruts carved in the road seemed to smooth out gradually as the pair walked side by side, every stride bringing them closer to their destination. Stories from their pasts, quick-witted banter, and even the occasional comfortable silence filled the passing hours, bringing Mel and Ransom closer. Talk was easy, and it seemed almost natural to share details that otherwise would have been brushed off or evaded.

"The emotion on my parents' faces when I was taken—or I guess I should say the lack of emotion . . . I never knew how little I meant to them until that moment." Mel spoke as though she had left a decade ago. "They mean nothing to me now, but I must go back and beg my queen to reconsider. Only then will I be protected."

"But your queen was the one who traded you and the other maidens, correct?" Ransom interjected, concerned and a little confused.

Mel scrunched her eyebrows in her own chagrin and hesitated a moment. "I know it seems odd, but I don't blame the queen. She has an entire kingdom resting on her shoulders. Thousands of people look to her for not only guidance, but quite literally to sustain their lives. She acted out of diplomacy. My parents acted out of pure selfishness."

"I can't even imagine. Not to brag or anything, but my father loves me a lot. Like, a lot a lot. Sometimes even too much, but I guess that's better than other relationships." Ransom's voice faded as he glanced at Mel. "I didn't mean to." He stumbled over his words. "I apologize. That wasn't what I meant."

"No, it's fine," Mel responded, not at all offended. "I'm glad you have that kind of relationship with your father. I'm sure it made the decision to leave very difficult."

"If I'm honest, it really hasn't been easy. Especially since he was the only person I had ever known until I met you. But I'm a man now. I can't sit around forever, scared that something might happen. I'm ready to prevent instead of cower. Besides, I won't be gone forever. I can visit my old man anytime I'd like. He just doesn't realize that." Ransom shook his head slightly. "Poor old guy needs a hobby, or a friend. Some parents just can't let go at all. So which is better? Parents who push you out, or parents who hold you back?" He posed the question with no semblance of an answer.

The road curved to the right, skirting around a group of ancient elms, then widened, smoothing to a nice, flattened roadway. Ransom stopped, taken aback by the site of a few buildings appearing close by. Stillemäch slowly formed in front of them, distant but strong.

Little hovels on the outskirts of the city scattered here and there between odd-shaped fields, but as Ransom and Mel drew nearer to the south gates, the buildings progressively became larger, with better structure and quality. The homes also moved closer and closer together until, inside the stone wall of the city, all stood wall to wall, stretching upward. Uneven cobblestone streets webbed through the maze of buildings, barely providing narrow passage for all commonality, livestock, and commerce to flow.

"This is incredible," Ransom exclaimed in a light, breathless exhale. His azure eyes widened, soaking in the entirety that made up the conventional city. Commoners busily traipsed from house to shop, living side by side without the need to regard one another. Carts flowed in and out of the gates. One, loaded with wool, headed toward the center square, while another, heavily ladened with barrels of grain, departed. Amused, Mel watched amazement fill Ransom's eyes as he studied the working men and women.

"Ho! Outta the way," a voice called, and she sidestepped quickly, just in time to avoid collision with the oxen pulling the enormous load of barrels.

"Are all cities this busy?" he asked, reading every sign, observing every building. "Illustrations do nothing to capture detail. This place is so much more than I could have ever imagined!"

Mel glanced around, trying to soak in the same sensation of awe. "Yep, most cities are like this. Dirty . . ."

"That sculpture is exquisite," Ransom interrupted, unable to stop himself.

Mel gave a small chuckle. "That's a pile of rubbish in the alley," she explained. "Smelly . . ."

With that cue, Ransom sniffed. "Something sweet, a little fermented and earthy is in the air. Not unpleasant at all. What is the source?."

"Horses. That smell is horse dung." He looked at her in disbelief. "No, really. Look there." She pointed out in her defense. "That's where they pile what they scrape off the streets. I saw the peasants doing the same thing once when I walked among the people."

Mel's words were brushed off as something new presented itself. "Look! That must be the schoolhouse with so many little children." Ransom pointed to a small home, clearly in disrepair and overrun by small inhabitants. One exhausted woman held a screaming infant in her arms, looking worse for the wear.

"Wrong again! Schoolhouses are not stuck between cottages. That is just a very large, very busy family. Yep, typical city life here. Dirty, smelly, overpopulated . . ."

"I love it!" Ransom cut in again with enthusiasm.

Mel smiled and shook her head. "Well, if you love this, then you will certainly love Smarahav. Unlike anywhere else, our buildings are built for beauty as much as function. The landscapes around are breathtaking, and we actually take pride in appearance." She stopped suddenly.

"What is it? Is something wrong?" he asked, looking from side to side. The exuberance diminished slightly as he quickly tensed for any threat, trying to gauge the elements around.

Mel touched his arm as a way of putting the man at ease. "No, nothing's wrong. Well, nothing dangerous anyway. I just remembered what I'm wearing! I think it's time I turned back into a lady, don't you?" Large eyes scanned quickly until, not too far ahead, she spied a sign with lightly scrolled letters. *Modiste.* "Ah, there! A dressmaker. Would you mind? I feel like I'll have a better chance with my queen if I clean up a bit. This is the last thing I need before securing passage."

"Of course. I wouldn't want you to be mistaken for a guard . . . again. We both know how that turned out last time," Ransom teased.

Mel smiled back as her hand raised in reflex to rub the back of her head, though there was no longer any pain. She touched the leather wrapped tightly around her hair and pulled the end of the thong, releasing a thick cascade of midnight tresses. Pushing through the wild locks, she felt the spot where the small bump had been, inflicted by her companion only three days prior. With a sideways glance, she noticed Ransom watching her intensely. His grin was amused, but his eyes were apologetic. "Don't worry about it. I almost died yesterday, remember? A bump to the head was nothing compared to that fall, and thanks to you, I have no pain from either."

His grin grew bigger, and he raised a large hand to her head to caress the spot she had just felt herself. "You may be the only lady I have ever met, but I have a feeling that there are no others quite like you."

The look in his eyes was more than amusement now. It was deeper, more meaningful. The tips of his fingers lingered just a little longer, entangled in the thick cascade. Her heart skipped a beat, and in the next moment she realized she had stopped breathing. Willing her lungs to function, her next instinct was to create a wall. *We are from two different worlds, on two different paths. I am so close to getting back home, and he'll be joining the king's cavalry. Now is not the time to fall.*

Turning away, she continued walking forward, attempting to pull herself back to the present. Smiling wryly, she tried turning the fire between them into a light spark instead. "In a sky spattered with stars, I'm just another speck of light. Nothing special. There's a million more just like me."

The conversation lulled, and Mel was thankful for the hustle of the city that Ransom couldn't resist getting caught up in. Boots scraped along the unevenly smooth stones, and soon they stood in front of the small, well-kept dress shop. "I'll go in alone, if that's okay. Meet me down this road?"

Ransom responded with a hearty nod. "I have plenty to do that doesn't involve silks and laces. I'll be waiting in the square."

Mel turned to the door but swung back in a flash. "Oh, here. Would you hold this for me? I don't think the dressmaker would appreciate me having a weapon in the store. I'd like to appear as lady-like as possible." She bent over and slid the sleek dagger out of her dirty, worn out boot.

The knife was light and delicate, but he knew that through the leather sheath sat an incredibly sharp little blade. "Of course, my lady," he answered with a slight bow and thick sarcasm.

"See, I feel more regal already." With that she turned on her heel and slipped into the shop, leaving the young man behind.

Looking down, he slid the dagger into his pocket for safe keeping when he noticed something. On the hilt, where a circular emerald had been, there now sat an empty divot. "Hmm, that's strange. The stone must have come loose and fallen off." Immediately Ransom knew what to do, and he slowly turned, surveying the street.

Further down the cobblestones, more and more shops popped into view. Stacked logs and sawdust showed where to find a carpenter. Large textiles pointed to a weaver, hanging on rope line, swaying in the breeze. Down further still, a baker's fresh yeast bread was released from the kiln, allowing the heavy scents to escape and dance in the air. Ransom stood quite the distance away, but not far enough to prevent the alluring aroma from reaching his own nose, and wrapping most of the dank city air in its homemade embrace for a lingering second or two. Temptation dissipated with no apologies, and he spotted the shop he'd been searching for. Between the weaver and an apothecary sat a small, completely ordinary shop with a humble, neatly lettered sign: *Silversmith*.

✳ ✳ ✳

Several hours later, as the mid-afternoon sun beat on his shoulders, Ransom wandered through the square, thoroughly enjoying every tiny detail of each exotic and domestic booth. The city was grounded with many fine merchant establishments but also alive with traveling tradesmen and women who had set up spaces along the center of Stillemäch, as they did every market day.

Temporarily erected on one end of the square was a pen emitting squeals as piglets hopped over one another. Ransom smiled, observing their miniature curly tails waggle, listening to their high-pitched whines. Next to the young swine sat a weathered old woman straightening bundles of wool piled high, and beyond that awaited other booths, some more eye-catching than others. He saw intricately woven baskets, mounds of produce in a rainbow of colors, spices and herbs for those tempted by flavor, leather crafts, ribbons, tools, and more.

Intrigued by the scythes and other iron lined up neatly for sale, Ransom studied their handles as well as craftsmanship. Eyes lingered on the curvatures of a delicate set of shears, simple and mundane to most, but singular to a man who had never held such objects before. He remained focused while feet stepped sideways and slowly continued down the street. With thoughts occupied, he failed to look in his path. An unexpected pain jolted through his hip as he collided with something hard. The jolt threw Ransom off balance, sending the young man stumbling backward, crashing against the iron-laden table and sending tools into disarray.

"Watch where yer going," the large ironsmith shouted in irritation, scrambling to rearrange his wares on display.

Quickly, Ransom scrambled to straighten his mess. "I apologize. So very sorry. Let me help," he begged pardon, but the grumbling ironsmith shooed him hastily away.

Embarrassed, Ransom turned to examine his obstruction and saw an old handcart had stopped in his path. A weathered peddler crooned over the baubles. "My apologies, sir. Are your wares and trinkets all right?"

The old, haggard man with the dust of the road upon his clothes straightened, counted, and tended to each of his possessions in a delicate, fatherly manner. Clouded eyes swept up, filled with irritation. Immediately, vexation evaporated into calm, turning to amity in the blink of a cloudy eye. "Just fine, just fine, young lad. Ev'rything seems to still be intact. No broken pieces or missing parts." The man adjusted his small satchel sitting across his chest, patting to confirm that it, too, was undamaged.

Ransom smiled broadly. "I'm glad to hear it. I do apologize for running into you, sir. So many wonderful sites to see, I dare say I lose my focus every once in a while."

The old, worn out face went blank in a trance-like manner. Then in a snap the friendly eyes had a new look in them. Curiosity, maybe? "Son, if you think there is much to see here, just wait until you finally see the world!"

"Ransom!" A faint hail from across the square drew his attention and he turned, eyes landing on a lady. Somehow, the broad smile widened still.

She looked familiar, but at the same time she had completely transformed into a stranger. He had left his traveling companion at the door of the dress shop, covered in dirt and smeared with soot, dressed in used men's clothes with worn leather boots and a mess of hair on her head. Now, the lady approaching seemed to be a copy of that person, but without the grime, tangles, and rags. She glided across the cobblestone square, treading lightly on slipper-clad feet. The hem of her marigold gown, decorated with slight golden embroidery swirling along the edges, brushed the stones underfoot, swaying from side to side. Sweeping up to enfold perfectly around her waist, the material flowed in one continuous movement, rounding over the curves of her body and ending in a square cut neckline decorated in matching golden swirls. Continuing from the neck, the material flowed over her slight shoulders, enveloping the arms in warm yellow perfectly, and ending just over her wrists in a small peek-a-boo of cream and gold lace. Mel had Ransom's full attention as he studied her radiance.

Unexpectedly, the peddler reached out, grabbing Ransom's hand and shaking it heartily. "A lucky man could go his entire life without beholding such an exotic jewel," the aged voice reached Ransom's ears. "Good luck, lad." With that, the grip released and the man hobbled, on one good leg and one crooked, to the front of his cart, pulling forward while mumbling under his breath. The wooden wheels, worn and cracked, creaked as he made his way through the bustle of the crowd, then turned off to the side, disappearing from sight.

Ransom watched the wake of the peddler fill in as busy traders and perusers continued business, then turned back just in time to come face to face with Lady Imelda. "Why do you look so confused?" she asked with no preamble. "I told you I was a lady of the court, didn't I? You shouldn't be so surprised that I actually fit in a dress!"

Ransom's good-natured smile returned, and he gave a small laugh. "Oh, it's not you that I'm confused about. On that subject I know exactly how I feel." His face didn't change, but his eyes intensified for a second. Then he side stepped, offering an arm. "You look incredible. Is that acceptable for me to say?"

"Men aren't usually so forthright with their feelings, but I accept your compliment with gratitude," she replied, gladly taking the proffered arm.

"Shall we walk, then?" he asked, leading with a nudge.

"Why, thank you. I think we shall. I have about an hour before catching the northern coach." The news brought the pair back to reality all too quickly, dampening the spirit of the afternoon. Clearing her throat, Mel attempted to start the conversation again. "So, if you're not confused about my transformation, which I think is pretty good myself, what is puzzling you?"

Ransom hesitated. "That man. Did you see him?"

"You mean that peddler you were talking to? Yeah, why?" They passed a woman sitting on a small, neatly woven rug, strumming her mandolin softly. The melody carried lightly in the air, happily fading in and out of ear as the ebb and flow of the market continued unfazed.

"He said something about me finally seeing the world. It wasn't just the words, though. It's the way he said them, like he knows something others don't. It was the strangest feeling, but of course it was completely unfounded. I never met the man in my life. Maybe the excitement of the day is wearing on me." Shaking his head to regain his usual carefree composure, he tilted down to look in the deep brown eyes that studied his face. "If I'm confused, I'm glad I have you to keep me upright."

The earthy yellow of the simple gown accented the warm tones of her skin, and Ransom noticed amber specked in her eyes. *Amber, a rare gemstone, like the one that used to be in the dagger's hilt.* "Oh, hey, I have something for you. Let's find a better place first." He looked from side to side, then veered off the main square, down a side street that ended at the base of a building. Ornate and magnanimous, yet quiet and still, the cathedral was a perfect setting for the couple's last hour. With Mel on his arm, they followed a solemn group of nuns walking toward their home.

Climbing the steps, the ladies of faith entered the enormous, intricately carved doors, but Ransom and Imelda reached the steps and turned, lowering down to sit side by side. The lack of scents and sounds was in complete contrast to the carnival-like atmosphere only a few blocks away, creating the perfect setting for what he had in mind.

"Wow," Mel sighed, more than a little impressed with the emphatic reverence in the air. "Now this is incredible. I've heard of Stillemäch's Great Cathedral before. It truly is something to behold." Her eyes sparkled as she studied the architecture over her shoulder.

Ransom memorized every perfect detail of the lady beside him, just as in awe. Finally, he cleared his throat. "Mel. I know you're leaving. I just want you to know how much I appreciate you being here with me. You nearly got caught again, even almost died, just because I forced you to come. I'm so very sorry." Mel began to argue, but Ransom continued. "I noticed the hilt on your dagger was missing the center stone."

"It was?" Mel asked, trying to guess where this was going.

The easy half-smile appeared, and the dimple returned to his cheek. "It was. It must have fallen off. Well, I hope you don't mind, but I took the liberty to . . ." Pulling the knife from his pocket, he passed it over to the dainty open palms. A small, involuntary gasp escaped her lips. There, covering the empty indention was a miniature silver dome. Half a spherical locket. A tiny hinge sat to one side, and she opened the miniature door, releasing beams of light that brightened her face, gentle and bright. Inside, sitting comfortably in the wooden and rosemary cage was the singular star speck glowing softly. Ransom watched with anticipation as she examined the gift. "We made it to my destination, but you still have to travel home. I figured you could use the star now."

Big eyes peeled from the glorious gift to peer up, glistening from tears not yet fallen. "This is the most thoughtful, incredible gift I have ever received," she stammered.

Laughter unexpectedly erupted from her throat, lifting the mood from intimacy to lightheartedness, and Ransom' eyes darted from the dagger to Mel and back again. "What? Is the locket on crooked or something?"

"No!" Mel quickly sobered. "There is absolutely nothing wrong with this gift. It is perfect. I'm only laughing because I got you something as well." Reaching into the pocket in her dress, she pulled out a large, beautiful square of crimson silk. "I got this for you. Actually, I pried the emerald off of the hilt of my dagger so I could buy it along with my dress." Draping the fabric over her palm, the corners cascaded, reflecting the sun like a bowl of polished rubies. Mel gave another awkward laugh. "I actually purchased it so you can wrap the star cage in something soft and delicate, and wear it in your pocket as a . . . a favor."

Ransom eyebrows raise in hopeful question. "A favor?"

"Well, yeah. It's customary for a soldier to wear a favor given to him by, well, by his lady." Her olive complexion turned a few shades rosier, and she quickly stopped.

He lifted the smooth silk from her hand, caressing the gift delicately. "Favor from my lady, huh? I like that idea." Their eyes met, and the flush on her face lightened slightly.

Her mouth tweaked into an ironic grin. "But it doesn't matter now since the star is in my hilt."

"How about this: you keep the star in the hilt for now. Then, the next time we see each other I'll take it." The red square was reverently folded. "In the meantime, I'll keep this silk, alone, as my favor."

"When will we see each other again?" The words caught in her throat, and she stopped herself before it wavered.

Ransom leaned over, close enough to share a breath. "I don't know about you, but I'm not ready for this to end."

Without thinking, Imelda closed the gap between them, pressing her lips gently, then firmly, against his. Instantly the gesture was returned, and he pressed back with the heat of a blazing fire. The kiss only lasted a moment, and then both pulled back slightly. He rested his forehead against hers and whispered, "I don't have to be a soldier."

Mel backed away farther. "Of course you do! You've been waiting your whole life for this. No, you have to go. Complete your training. Do what you came to do. Fulfill your destiny. I'll be waiting on the Emerald Isle until you return." He leaned closer to the beautiful maiden at his side, and Mel laid her head on his strong shoulder. "Love can wait a little longer."

20

A PEDDLER'S TRICK

Stone steps remained cool as the sun continued on its course. Muffled sounds of the busy square danced in the distance. With so much left unseen, Ransom expected to feel a pull into the excitement of the crowd, yet his body relaxed into Mel's, cemented to the steps of the ancient cathedral. His arms tightened around her frame, curves molding to his side like the missing half to his puzzle, and the perfumed head rested lightly on his shoulder, dark strands catching sunlight with every subtle shift. Traces of vanilla rose wafted ever so slightly, and Ransom inhaled the deeply rich scents, smiling. *Lovely, but if I had to choose I'd pick the earthy scents from our time in the forest.*

Enrobed in the stunning yet simple marigold dress, the stillness synchronized their hearts into one beat. Muscles tightened around the back of her waist, and every thought of parting pulled her a little closer. His other large hand rested between her much smaller palms, both gently holding firm, as though their grip could slow time. Finally, Ransom reluctantly released the maiden. "It's time, Mel," he declared, pushing himself off the steps and offering his hand to the waiting lady. The light in his eyes dimmed, matching her own discomfort and pain, and she accepted the proffered hand, drawing herself closer to his body. Gentle fingers slid onto his face, feeling the tight, smooth skin, and rested on the strong jaw. Silently he bowed to meet her brow again. One more moment, one more understanding. Tilting his head to the side, she moved automatically. They shared one more kiss in this sanctuary. Out of duty, not desire, Ransom pulled away but continued to clutch her hand, wordlessly turning, and she matched his grip, walking by his side.

They made their way back up the quiet street, the volume of the square increasing with every step. One more footfall took the couple back into the hubbub of the market and Ransom's stride quickened. "We'd better move quickly," he all but shouted over his shoulder, weaving through the bustling crowd. "I don't think we have the luxury of time if you're going to make it to the northern carriage."

Mel smiled, but humor failed to reach her eyes. Mixed emotions vied for attention, and all she could do was squeeze his hand in response. Together, they cut across the center of the square, pushing between sturdy booths until their feet followed another narrow street of stones.

The ache in his chest threatened to take control as the pair arrived all too soon at the carriage house. Sturdy, weather-worn doors sat open, and though they were ajar, the dim interior was anything but welcoming. To the side, stables were wild with life as horses of all breeds and sizes were housed for short stints. Though just as busy as the square, new sounds and smells filled the air with every hoof kicking up straw and earth, creating a wilder atmosphere thick with animal excitement.

Together, the couple entered the dim space of the carriage house, the crunch of straw underfoot punctuating each step. At first glance the place appeared vacant, but as Ransom scanned, Mel cleared her throat, jabbing slightly at her companion's side and nodding toward the far corner. There, propped on a milking stool while leaning against a rough-looking pillar rested a man covered in the grime of a half-day's labor.

"Excuse me," Ransom hailed, unable to wait for the man to conclude his interlude on his own. The man stirred and Ransom tried again. "Pardon us, sir." The man came to with a start. "We're seeking a carriage heading north."

"North?" the crabby stable keeper asked, irritated by the unexpected interruption. Grumbling, gurgling sounds could be heard as he sat up and spat into the graying straw. "Yeah," he croaked, his voice cracking and dry, "we got a carriage scheduled fer north. Coming 'round any time now, but there ain't no room fer two."

"No problem," Ransom responded, good-natured but firm. "We won't be needing two seats. However, we're hoping you'll have room for one."

The man spat again, wiping his chin with a dingy yellowed sleeve. "Nah, young man. Ain't got a spot fer ya. Ye'll have'ta find yer own way."

"You misunderstand, good sir. The seat isn't for me. It's for the lady," Ransom stated, gesturing toward the maiden at his side.

Mel stepped forward with her chin held high. The stable keeper's eyes widened. "Um-hm." He quickly cleared his throat, red face turning scarlet. "I recall now, might've misspoke. Ah yes, one seat does sit free. Me mind muddles from time to time. The lady is welcome te ride." His eyes darted back to Ransom, narrowing. "Ye do have coin?"

Wanting to spend as little time with this surly man as possible, Mel turned and headed out the door, happy to wait outside. "Of course," Ransom responded. "You'll receive payment in full upon the lady's safe arrival in Smarahav." The scowl soured on the filthy man's face as Ransom followed out of the carriage house.

A myriad of emotions surged through her veins as Mel shuffled back and forth, creating a slightly worn path in the packed earth. "I guess you're all set now," Ransom declared, the cheer in his voice a little forced. "Oh, I almost forgot." Mel stopped moving, feeling the overwhelming anxiety ebb with him by her side. Ransom reached into his satchel, retrieving the large emerald necklace. "I didn't mean to keep this for so long. You'll be needing it to pay for the ride home."

A quick, dull pain pulsed through her heart as the word *home* escaped his lips. *Am I really headed toward home? Or am I leaving it?* His fingers gently wrapped around her hand, lifted it palm up, and lowered the emerald with the thick chain. As her fingers closed around the cold metal, she realized that the weight was heavier now than it had a few days before. "Ransom?"

"Look, Mel," he interrupted, his smile mismatching the sadness in his eyes. "You helped me get to where I needed. I'm not going to stop you from doing the same. Like we said, we'll see each other again. Go win your life back. Just save a spot for me once you have."

Mel pushed herself up on her toes and pressed her lips firmly against Ransom's one last time. Without another word, she shuffled back, turning to the stables. "Goodbye, Mel," Ransom said softly, the words weighted with emotion. Knowing that lingering wouldn't stop the longing, he turned toward the western side of the city where the palace courtyard awaited, and where the royal guards were sure to be.

* * *

Following the maze of bylanes, he made his way toward Castle Stillemäch. The streets were quieter, muffled as brick and mortar replaced the open wooden booths of the square. Though the commerce in these parts seemed more frivolous than the necessary wares of the market, Ransom could not deny the feeling of importance, as if simply being closer to the castle automatically bestowed significance. Whether it was just in his head or a tangible reverberation, the young, duty bound man walked a little straighter, chest raised, adopting an air that meant business.

Royal walls surrounding the courtyard grew larger and larger until Ransom felt dwarfed in comparison to the sheer size and fortitude of the structure. Beyond the wall, past the courtyard, the castle stood in magnificent glory. *Castle Stillemäch.* A strange pull beckoned, and Ransom felt as though he had been there before. Impossible, yet undeniable. Taking a deep breath, he stepped forward.

"You would leave and join the force of strangers without saying goodbye to the only person you have ever known?" Draven emerged from the shadows, stepping slowly, deliberately, keeping his back to the royal grounds. The once agile hunter stood withered and worn, only a shell of what he had been just a few days back.

"Father . . . I . . . well . . ." the young man stammered.

Draven shuffled forward, achy and exhausted. His shallow breath was labored, but his eyes, though surrounded in creases, were as sharp and intense as a circling buzzard's. "Ransom, Ransom, stop your blathering. It's all right. I finally understand. Really, I do. You feel drawn to this place, like you have a higher purpose. I didn't see it before, but I do now. I just wanted to come say goodbye, have a drink with my son, and wish him farewell. Would you at least allow me that?"

Ransom's rigid stature, tense and on guard, relaxed little by little, his muscles loosening as his shoulders lowered. His square jaw eased as his sandy brows turned from furrowed to raised, then softened into a comfortable familiarity. "Of course, Father," he replied, heart warming easily to his only family in the entire world. "I would love, more than anything, to have one more drink with you."

"Excellent. There's a little place this way." A weakened, wrinkled hand rested on Ransom's shoulder and steered the young man from the royal yard. Not one to resist his father's will, he allowed the aging man to steer him along, but not without looking over his shoulder. All that remained visible of the mighty castle were the spires stretching high beyond the solid wall. *Soon*, he thought to himself, *my new life starts soon.* In the subdued atmosphere of the castle boundaries, a faint, muffled creaking followed behind.

✳ ✳ ✳

"To my son! Loyal and dutiful to a fault. May he remain so forever." Draven's scratchy voice was hardly heard by any other patron in the tavern, but the toast was only meant for one.

Feeling himself slipping into old habits of submission and apologies, Ransom worked against succumbing to ingrained patterns. A usual bow of the head would follow by now, but he held his chin high. "Thank you, Father, and may good health and longevity always lay at your door."

Draven gave a wicked smile behind his tankard. "Oh, I plan on it," he stated softly before drinking. Ransom took a swig as well, and the world immediately transformed. Hit with a swirling feeling in the pit of his stomach, the floor began to tilt. *Something is wrong. The drink. Poison.* Thoughts raced through his head as Ransom struggled to take back control over his mind and body, but the poison moved too quickly, already numbing his limbs as well as his thoughts. Draven slid his chair back slowly, lifting himself from his seat with immense difficulty, and shuffled around the small table to stand behind his prize.

"You think you can take my power from me?" the withered man hissed in his ear. "I stole you eighteen years ago, and I am not about to let you go now. As my son or as my prisoner, you will never leave the tower again." Weak, wrinkled hands rested on the young man's sloping frame. Ransom barely heard the whispered chant but felt the surge of power leave his body as renewed strength extended to the tips of the fingers on his shoulders. Everything visible wavered, blossoming into a fog, darkening, spreading incredibly fast, and for the first time in his life Ransom felt weak. Willpower was no match for the paralyzing effects seeping through his body. Then, like the sudden breath extinguishing the flame of a midnight candle, blackness engulfed him.

✳ ✳ ✳

"Excuse me, Monsieur, could you please tell me when the carriage will be here?"

The irritable stable keeper huffed and stomped about, hauling reins and pitching straw. "It'll git here when it gits here," he responded for the umpteenth time.

Exasperated, Mel paced in front of the large doors. Her hands returned to hips like a magnet, anxiety returning. "Four hours!" she complained to the empty streets and stabled companions. "I should have been gone four hours ago." The horses did little more than turn an ear to acknowledge the burst of frustration, having become accustomed to the lady who was clearly out of place. Her legs finally begged for respite from the never-ending pacing, and reluctantly Mel surveyed the area for a decent place to rest. Spotting several barrels near the stockyard, she stomped over and fanned her skirt out as she lowered down. As the thick marigold skirt fell on top of her thighs, something hard scraped dully against her flesh, and she reached into the pocket to extract the dagger in its leather sheath. Her heart skipped a beat. Cradling it in one hand, her fingers gently caressed the perfect little locket door on the hilt of her trusty knife. Prying slightly, no light seeped through the crack. Opening it wide, the star could be seen resting dark and dormant, cold as a speck of ordinary granite. Rudely interrupting the moment, four brindled mares pulled in, harnessed to a large carriage and ready for their long journey ahead. They halted when the reins were drawn and command was given, standing as still as one would expect from a well trained, excited team. Finally, she was able to return home but felt no relief as the dagger remained heavy in her hand. Turning away, Mel stood up and walked a few steps down the cobblestones, following Ransom's invisible trail. Instantly the speck began to glow, lightly but unmistakable.

The coachman, just as caked in grime as his business partner, spat a few hurried words at his friend. With a nod, the keeper turned to the waiting lady.

"Ahem!" he called out impatiently. "Your carriage, my lady." The words croaked through clenched teeth.

Returning to the carriage, eyes remained on her hilt. The glow in the locket faded to nothing. *It will lead me to where I need to be. Home. Smarahav is no longer my home, nor is any place. The only time I have ever truly felt like myself, felt like I was home, was when I was with . . .*

A high-pitched screech interrupted the thought, and Mel searched the sky for the black silhouette of a falcon against the blue. "Ransom," she gasped, securing the little locket closed with a snap. The coachman and keeper waited with a combination of expectation and confusion. The small carriage door remained open, but instead of entering, she backed away. "I apologize, but I cannot travel today. Maybe never. I was already where I needed to be." Quickly, she turned, leaving two irritated, stunned men behind.

On slippered heels, she raced down the cobblestones in a flurry of rich yellow. *He may have already joined the ranks of the cavalry, but I can still be with him. If I can't, I'll wait here, where he'll return. Either way, he needs to know that I'm not going anywhere.* The palace courtyard raised in sight, and she flew as fast as her feet could carry her. Her hair flew back in a sheet of black, bouncing with every step. *Nothing can stop me.*

The clatter and racket of precious goods reverberated strangely as an old man stepped straight into her path, pulling a wooden cart quickly. The antique trinkets protested, jostling wildly while he purposely cut her off. Surprised, she skittered to a halt, nearly crashing into both man and cart, but in doing so caught a slipper-clad toe on the hem of her dress. Without warning, she fell hard onto her knee, the crack of bone against solid rock snapping quick and sharp. Gasping, Mel was blinded by pain for a moment.

"Dear me, dear me," and old, withered voice mumbled at her side. "A nasty fall, if ye don't mind me saying, my lady."

She looked up to see the old crooked man from the square offering a hand. "You?" she exclaimed, hurt and confused. "What were you . . . Who . . . ?"

"Please, mademoiselle, we don't have much time," he interrupted, hand still offered. Wanting to pull away from the travel-worn stranger, something pulled her in. Reluctantly, she grabbed a hold of his wrinkled hand, begrudgingly grateful for the assistance. The sting of the fall spread like a web of fire over her knee and she squinted in pain, fighting the urge to cry out. "My name is Torban. I am a merchant wanderer, a peddler and acquirer of rare commodities. Magical commodities."

He paused to allow the information to soak in, but the distraction of the injury slowed her capabilities. "Why are you telling me all this?" she asked, looking past the man toward the palace yard.

Torban pressed on. "I have a special ability to detect magic in otherwise seemingly ordinary objects, and people." Mel's eyes quickly snapped from the courtyard to the weathered man, but she said nothing.

"I know about your friend, my lady. The young man has strong magic running through his veins. The strength of a mountain, to be exact. I also know that he is not safe. Sitting here as I was, inconspicuous and such, I seen your friend approach the gates, but before he entered, an old, wicked man approached and persuaded the lad to have a farewell drink. Your friend called him Father."

"You mean, Ransom never made it in?" Panic rose in her voice, the pain in her leg put aside. "Which way did he go?"

"Down that away, into a tavern. I felt something curious so took liberties to follow. Didn't want to be seen though, and didn't have no coins, so I stayed on the street in wait. Not too long after, the same gentleman came out the building supporting the lad 'round his waist and letting him lean over shoulder. Oh he was loud enough, spouting out how some need to learn to hold their drink. The thing is, the man was no longer the same graying fellow that had gone in. Oh, he was the same man all right, but had reversed his years some forty-ought, and I fine'ly recognized the sly fox. Ye see, I've done a bit of business with that man. Not one to trifle with."

"But where is he now?" Mel asked again, desperate for a direction.

"Loaded onto the back of a wagon. Poor guy was dead to the world, and the fox drove off as quickly as if he set fire to the castle!" A cannon fired its first shot of tribute. "My lady, yer man is no ordinary man . . ."

Imelda studied the old peddler cautiously. "No, he's not, but you've already said that."

"No, my lady. Yer man is a prince. The firstborn to King Barrett and Queen Felicity. I'd know that kind of power anywhere. The Lost Prince of Stillemäch. The thief that stole that baby was never found, but I have a feeling he'll make sure he's twice as hidden now."

Another screech sounded, high pitched and far away, but as Mel looked up, the silhouette she expected to see in the distant blue skies floated closer and closer until the beautiful bird landed directly on her shoulder. Uncharacteristically, Valk nipped softly at her ear, nuzzling the feathers atop her head against Mel's cheek, flapping anxiously. "I know, Valk. Ransom's gone, but we'll get him back," Mel cooed to the bird, then turned back to Torban in haste. "I have to go."

"Go already?" A soft, unfamiliar voice beckoned from the entrance of the castle yard. Both Mel and Torban's eyes snapped in the same direction as the young lady dressed in a simple gown of vintage rose approached silent but quick, feet floating easily over the cobblestones. A cream parasol hovered low, almost resting on top of her head, concealing the identity of this high-born stranger. "Please!" she called out again. "Please, I'd love to have a word."

As the lady came face to face with the odd pair, the parasol tilted up to reveal a young, round face with large, curious eyes and a wide pink smile. Though time could not be spared, Mel's feet stood rooted, drawn to the unfamiliar face but strangely familiar eyes. Immediately, Torban bent as low as an old back was capable, head bowing in submission. "Your highness," the withered voice cracked in surprise.

A slight dip of the young lady's head acknowledged what the peddler surmised. She then turned elegantly to face the lady in golden yellow. "I have been waiting days for your return to my city. A true Smarahavie lady! I have so much I'd love to discuss."

Mel quickly looked to the old man and back, dipping into an awkward curtsy. "Your highness, nothing would gave me more pleasure, but I must go. . ." Her breath cut short as the slight bend awakened the beast in her knee. The sentence finished with the hiss of air sucked in sharply through gritted teeth. Offended, Valk took flight, instead choosing to circle overhead.

The excited smile quickly melted into worry. "Oh dear, my lady, were you injured?" The young princess stepped forward, arms out, offering stability.

"I'm afraid so," Mel responded, nearly falling to the ground, "but it doesn't matter."

An old hand grabbed her forearm. "I shall mend that knee first." Though stated plainly, Torban's kind face gently questioned. Brows raised in confusion, but her body relaxed, giving a tiny nod. Another cannon shot boomed in the air. Turning to his cart, the peddler quickly rifled through the mess of knickknacks. "Aha," he exclaimed, pulling out an ordinary stick, worn smooth from use.

Wariness crept back up. "A stick?" Mel asked skeptically.

"Forgive me, but what would such a simple stick do for a hurt leg?" the princess asked while closing in. Her hand automatically reached for Mel's elbow to support it, as if the two were as familiar as long lost friends.

"No simple stick here, your highness. Now please, my lady, lift your skirts to the knee, and lend me yer injury." Torban paused, absentmindedly wracking his brain, "Now, let's see, what are the words? Hibbi-di-hobbidi-hoo? No, that sounds like something a young owl would do. Pibbidi-pobbidi-poo! Well, that's not right, now is it? And frankly a little offensive."

Mel sighed deeply. "I really must go," she pronounced again, pulling her arm from the support and attempting to hobble away.

"Ah yes. Bibbidi-bobbidi-boo!" Instantly, a spark flew through the air, enrobing the exposed leg in momentary light, and just as quickly, the web of pain ceased. The ugly purple already spreading across her knee quickly receded as she bent her leg. Both pairs of brown and blue eyes turned to the withered man in sheer amazement.

"Thank you!" Mel gasped, marveling at the results, nearly forgetting the urgency of the hour. A screech from above pulled her back into focus. "Thank you, sir! Thank you so much." Backing away from the unlikely pair on the street, Mel turned to go.

"My lady," the old voice hailed, "another hand might do ye well."

Mel shook her head. "I apologize, sir, but you'll only slow me down."

"Not me. Oh no, but what about a sister? Ransom can use all the help he can get now."

Audrei's heart dropped to the pit of her stomach as she heard the name of the Lost Prince. Her own brother. "What do you mean?"

With no time left to spare, Mel simply nodded. "It's true. Will you come?"

Wide eyes as blue as the sky jumped back and forth between the two strangers, heart gaining speed. With a quick glance over her shoulder, all she saw were thick, stone walls, and she turned to face the adventure. Trusting her instincts, Audrei gave one solid nod.

"Come on! I'll explain on the way," Mel called as both ladies gathered their skirts just above the ankles.

Torban waved them off. "Please, go! Save that man that you love."

"Love?" The word caught Mel off guard, and she stood for a brief moment, looking at the peddler dumbstruck and confused.

The old, dry lips turned up in a knowing smile. "I told ye, my dear. I have uh gift fer spotting magic." With that the old man gathered his cart under his arms. Stubborn wheels creaked, turning down the lane.

"Come on," Mel called as the two ladies propelled over the cobblestones in slippered feet. Though the distance wasn't far, the heat of the evening and heavy-layered dresses added to the strenuous sprint. Still, the two ran un-ladylike, life itself depending on their efforts.

Arriving back at the stables, chests heaved deeply and tumbling hair fell out of place, framing flushed cheeks. The sudden appearance of two ladies on a mission startled the stable keeper, who was back on his milking stool, just easing into another nap. Pulling the necklace from her pocket, Mel tossed the expensive piece at the wide-eyed man. "I need horses. Now!"

Within no time, they kicked the muscular sides of two strong chocolate mares, leaving behind a grimy, bewildered man with a slight half-smile, staring into the facets of an enormous green gemstone. Raven and corn silk hair flew in the wind, marigold and rose cascading over the powerful flanks as they steered the horses into the forest, dodging branches and hurling through webs of thin boughs. Thick hooves drummed powerfully on the solid earth, but Audrei's excited and Mel's terrified hearts beat louder.

21

OBEDIENCE, LOYALTY, AND LOVE

Pure blackness faded into shades of gray, lightening in swirls as he attempted to make sense of his surroundings. Slowly, the heavy smoke lifted enough to finally crack open an eye. *Stone.* Stone walls, stone floor, stone heart. The tower hadn't changed, and why would it? He was only gone for a few days, although it felt like a lifetime. *How have I let myself stay a prisoner inside this enormous cage? What possessed me to stay as long as I have?*

Obedience. Loyalty. Love. All the virtues a good son should have. He did everything he had been asked, without question, never requiring anything in return. Now, he sat as a prisoner again. Ransom tried to rise but was restricted. Powerful muscles flexed as he summoned the strength of a mountain, and still nothing happened. Nothing had never happened before. The rope remained taut around his body, keeping him bound and still. Feeling angry, hurt, and uncomfortably chilled on the unforgiving floor, the young man threw his head back in frustration, sending bits of rock flying from the wall behind.

"Careful. You wouldn't want to be knocked unconscious. Again." *The stone heart.* Draven waited in his usual chair, observing as the younger awakened. A triumphant expression covered his smooth face, like a hunter who finally got the best of an illusive trophy buck. "I really wish it never had to come to this, son, but you were the one that decided to change everything, not I."

Anger welled from deep inside and Ransom pushed again at his enchanted confines. "How could you do this? I am your son!" He paused. "*Was* your son." The words whispered in the tavern came back to mind. "I'm not your son. Never was. I was always just a prisoner, here to do your will."

"Yes, and it will remain that way forever. You will stay here, tied and tethered, until the end of time." Draven smirked, bitterness morphing into arrogant resolve. "Come tomorrow I shall go in search of a cloaking spell that will hide this tower once and for all."

Immediately Ransom's heart dipped into the pit of his stomach. *She's halfway to Smarahav by now, waiting for me to return and claim her hand. She'll be waiting forever.* The only thing keeping his heart from completely shattering into a million pieces was hope that she would tire of waiting, forget him, and find someone who would cherish her fighting spirit as much as he did. Forlorn, he bowed his head and whispered, "Mel."

"Ransom . . ." Her voice reached his memory, low, distant. At least he could remember the sound of her voice clearly. *I'll always remember it as such.* A high-pitched screech cut through the air, and Ransom looked up in surprise, spotting Valk in the sky through the frame of the solid window. The sight of his friend brought comfort. *I am not alone.* "Ransom . . ." He heard Mel's voice again, but this time closer.

Not the only one to hear the call, Ransom struggled against his restraints as Draven rose from his chair, quick on his ageless feet to peer out the window just as a beautiful woman burst into the clearing, holding tight. Her dark arms tensed and her eyes narrowed on the tower as her powerful steed gave everything to the cause. Black hair of both damsel and mare flew wildly in sync as the yellow dress spilled over the side of the powerful animal, appearing as though the sun itself were melting off its glistening, sweat-streaked back.

She came back! Helplessly, Ransom studied Draven with new eyes, finally understanding what the man was capable of. Breath became shallow as a myriad of emotions threatened to suffocate, and he fought the urge to both smile and panic. *She can't be here. Draven won't let her live, but I won't let him hurt her.* His eyes darted around, searching for anything he could use to free himself. *I have to stop her. Tell her to leave. Something.*

With no hope of loosing his binds in time, panic won out. "Mel! Don't . . ." Ransom choked on the words as a crimson scarf whipped around his mouth, tied hastily but efficient. Draven stepped from the side and walked back to the open frame. This time he wasn't empty handed. The soft, scratching sound of a dragging pick ax across the stone floor turned Ransom's stomach inside out. The hunter peered over the ledge, watching Imelda dismount the huffing beast and approach the greenery that hung from the highest window.

"Ransom!" she shouted again, finally reaching the west end. "Are you there? Please answer. Ransom!" Small, shaking hands reached for the thickest vine, tugging to check stability. *No more thinking. I have to get up there.* Bracing against the wall as she had done before, Mel leaned back slightly, stepping one vertical step in front of the other. She scaled the wall, slow but steady, her dress trailing behind in the breeze. Her slippers had less grip than soldier's boots, but at least her footwear fit snugly this time, creating a more sure footing. One hand above the other, putting her whole heart into the effort, she continued without regard to her own safety, knowing danger could be waiting above.

Draven watched over the ledge, observing Mel as she struggled up the thick vines. "Time to end this," he stated simply, cold as the stone he stood upon. Ransom struggled with all his might but was unable to move and unable to yell. With no more hesitation, the older man lifted the heavy ax over his shoulder and swung, swift and steady. The tip of the sharp iron crashed full force onto the window ledge, splitting the vine and sending shards down onto the dark beauty's head. She paused her efforts, feeling the vibration of the hit, and looked up just in time to see stones raining from above. Crouching quickly, she braced herself, narrowly missing the large solid blocks. As the loose stones eased up overhead, she chanced another glance, terror striking in her heart like a bolt of iced lightning. In that instant the head of the pick ax swung down with fury. Vines shook as larger stones descended, one the size of a fist tearing into her shoulder. Helplessly, she cried out in pain, tightening her failing grip on the leafy rope. Thinking quickly, she began to reverse in a desperate attempt to flee. As fast as possible, her hands moved, one under the other, as Mel tried to steady tired muscles, strained from supporting her own weight for so long.

Draven swung the ax again and the vine snapped, going slack in her hands, and the world became a blur. She fell, letting out an involuntary scream before landing with a hard thud on the hidden platform below. The impact knocked the breath from her lungs, but a rock knocked the lights out. Standing on the windowsill high above, Draven smiled down at the sight of the woman sprawled on the ground. "Now there are no more vines to climb. No way for anyone to ever bother us up here again." He turned from the sill, releasing the ax, and walked over to his prisoner to untie the silk gag. "Don't worry, she might not be dead, though she had quite the fall." Just as he spoke, the windowsill crumbled on its own, continuing the job that had been started. Without warning, the entire ledge broke apart, falling in an avalanche of stones.

Already unconscious, Mel lay as still as a carved granite statue, unable to protect herself from the wrath raining above. Debris crashed mercilessly into a heap, piling on top of her unmoving body. From above, the ground directly below was no longer green and lush, but rather varying shades of gray piled and scattered around with bits of marigold peeking through the cracks.

"Imelda!" Ransom cried, although the girl could not answer. "Mel!" A culmination of feelings fought for recognition: panic, fury, longing, and sorrow. He struggled against his restraints harder than ever.

"Don't bother," Draven stated arrogantly. "Now she is dead. If the fall didn't kill her, surely the stones did. I warned you that people are bad, and now look what she has done to you. She hurt you, son. Love always ends in sorrow."

"Don't call me that. I am not your son." The ripping pain in his heart was blinding, but he choked it down to focus. *There might still be a chance. Not a chance of freedom, but a chance to save Mel one final time.* "I'll never be your son again, but I will swear to being your prisoner. Forever. Just as you want. No need for rope, or chains, or walls for that matter. I will swear allegiance and obedience only to you as my master, if . . ."

"If?" The excitement of greed grew more and more obvious in Draven's eyes.

"If you let me save her." Ransom saw skepticism wash over his captor's face and continued quickly. "She might not be dead yet. Let me climb down and check for life, heal her, then bid goodbye forever."

Draven paced, thinking rapidly as there was no time to spare. "No, no, I cannot do that. Too risky."

"I have been nothing but loyal and obedient my entire life. Completely unwavering. Haven't I earned any trust at all? I give you my word. If you let me heal her, I will stay your prisoner, willingly, forever." Ransom paused, seeing that he still wasn't getting through to Draven. "If you don't," he continued, his voice turning dark and forceful, "I will fight you every second of every day. I will constantly look for ways to escape. Once I do—and you know someday I will—the vengeance I wield will be great."

With no other way, Draven walked over hesitantly. "Give me your word."

Ransom stared back, chin high and strong. "I will not fight. I pledge my life to you."

With that, Draven untied the magic rope, unwinding it from Ransom's wrists, allowing it to slacken and fall around his body. Immediately Ransom burst forward, squelching his instincts to kill Draven on the spot, and ran to the crumbled window ledge. Below, so far away, the yellow peeked out of the scattered gray. She might be dead, but he was not willing to accept it so easily. Craning his neck, Ransom searched for a vine long enough, but all had been cut, severed, and splintered, heaped on the ground as part of the disarray decorating the meadow below. Desperately he turned, searching the tower for something long and strong enough.

Draven watched the younger man flounder. "Don't bother. I made sure there was nothing to use long ago, but since we have a bargain, I am a man of my word and you will have the opportunity to save that girl, *if* she is still alive." He moved toward the hallway, stopped, and haled over his shoulder, "Are you going to keep searching for something that's not there, or are you going to climb down the tower?"

Ransom knew he had no other options except to trust the evil man. Following him down the hallway, they entered the bedchamber. Ransom looked about with a mixture of guarded urgency and confusion as Draven stopped beside the bed. "Move this," the older man commanded.

Without giving voice to the hundreds of questions in his head, Ransom walked to the side of his bed and pushed easily. The heavy frame slid to the side, revealing a hidden door recessed in the floor. With no time to register shock and disbelief—there would be time for all that later—he bent down with relief, ripping open the door and plunging into darkness.

※ ※ ※

Emerging from the dank, narrow staircase, Ransom blinked through the blinding sunlight but never stopped moving. He rounded the tower, running at full speed until coming to a crashing halt by the heap of fallen stones. Finally, his eyes adjusted fully, and all he could focus on was the yellow playing peekaboo from underneath. Springing into action, Ransom lifted rocks off of the body of the crushed maiden, working quickly, and soon he had her uncovered, though the results of the stones left behind a pitiful sight.

Countless bones lay broken, though unseen beneath the tattered dress. Legs splayed out from the fall, one arm spread wide, away from the body, while the other bent inward beside her damaged frame. Seeping from a large gash, bright red blood adorned her beautiful face just below the hairline. Another channel of red cut through the side of her jawline, along with darkening purple spreading from eye to chin. "Mel! Imelda!" Ransom called, urgent but gentle as he ran his palm softly over the wild hair. "Are you still here? Please. Don't go. I'm so sorry." All he needed was a tiny sign that life still pulsed somewhere inside. Anything.

Fighting the darkness that closed in, full, dry lips barely parted. "Lost Prince." She forced the words from her throat with one of her last shallow breaths.

His heart leapt in gratitude. He held his hand to the side of her face, shielding the sun's blinding rays from her eyes, and spoke soft and low. "I know, I know. I'm the Lost Prince. Shh, it's all right. I'm going to heal you like before. You'll go far from here and live a safe, happy life. I just can't come with you."

Imelda struggled to speak again, the words catching deep in her parched throat. Long, black lashes lifted from her cheeks, and she looked at Ransom through her deep brown eyes one last time. "I love you." The words were barely audible, fading in the soft breeze. Summoning all her strength, quick as a rattlesnake strike, her hand swung up from her side, wielding the small dagger in her grip, and, in one quick motion, pierced the hand that shaded her eyes. The blade sank deep into his palm, and Ransom instantly felt the release of power as he fell back, resting on rough knees. He lifted his hand, gripping the wrist to hold steady while his own blood flowed in small streams down his forearm, dripping to the ground.

A faraway *No!* came from above, and Ransom turned to see horror consume Draven's face as the man registered what had happened. Observing from the largest window in the tower, the mask of horrified shock melted as Draven's skin began to transform, loosening with every second. The dark, thick hair on his head faded, lightening and thinning rapidly until it all fell in wisps of nothingness. His muscles softened and shrank as bones pressed through, the stature of his frame changing from tall and strong to weak, frail, and slumped. Rapidly, all color faded from the man in the window, all flesh, and all life until skeletal remains fell forward, plummeting skull first toward the ground far below. As the bones descended, they continued to age their natural progression, disintegrating before Ransom's eyes until, halfway down, the last of the bone dust whisked away in the breeze.

Gritting his teeth, Ransom pulled the blade from his palm, grabbed the crimson cloth still tied around his neck, and wrapped the gaping hole securely.

"Mel?" a timid voice called from behind, urgent and unsure. He turned quickly, raising his eyes to behold a young woman approaching, golden tresses reflecting the evening sun. "Is she . . ."

Turning his back to the stranger, he leaned over Imelda protectively, watching as life faded from her broken body. With the role of healer stripped from his being, he could only act as comforter now. With a heavy, broken heart he accepted his job at her side.

Audrei approached solemnly, kneeling across from the young man, beside Mel's head, heart breaking at the loss of her new, brave friend. "She was incredible," she whispered, resting a hand lightly on the tattered shoulder.

Ransom nodded slightly, smoothing the dark hair again. Breaths became increasingly shallow. "Of the billion stars in the sky"—he spoke to the broken beauty gently, barely able to keep his voice steady—"you were the North Star, Mel. I'd be lost without you. You saved me. Please, don't leave now." He bent forward so their lips were barely a nail head apart, and, knowing his words couldn't change anything this time, he hoped they could at least bring her peace as he whispered, "You are the strength in my marrow, you are the strength in my bones. If time were reversed, I'd gladly stand alone. Recover, revive, redeem, renew. Bring back the person that I once knew." Immediately, he lowered his lips to hers, gently bestowing one last kiss.

A burst of power surged, but not from the man of the tower. A radiance beamed from the princess, flowing from the tips of her fingers, flooding the limp, near lifeless body. Gradually, a transformation rolled over Mel's cold, still frame, spreading to the tips of her limbs. Fading from angry purple, her face restored itself to a healthy glow. Jagged, torn flesh moved slowly together until the edges bound, becoming perfectly seamless and smooth. Warmth returned as her heart resumed its normal rhythm, beating regular and strong. Bones shifted into place, and other unseen injuries righted themselves until she lay as the most perfect form of herself.

Ransom and Audrei watched in amazement as Mel came back to them. Finally, Audrei lifted her hand from the marigold shoulder and looked to Ransom for an answer. At the same moment Ransom truly looked at the young lady for the first time, and into eyes that mirrored his own. "How? My powers are gone. I felt them leave. I couldn't bring her back, even with my whole heart, but you did. Who are you?" he asked, grateful, confused, and searching.

"I don't know how. I've never felt that before in my life," Audrei responded softly, stunned and slightly lightheaded. "Maybe it's genetic."

"Genetic?" Ransom repeated, taken aback. "For it to be genetic you'd have to be . . ."

"Your sister." Round eyes glistened with every word. "I am, Ransom. If you are the Lost Prince, I am your sister, Princess Audrei of Stillemäch."

"Sister? I have a sister?" Ransom looked in the glossy blue eyes and saw the truth as plain as his own reflection.

A deep inhalation brought focus back to the dark beauty in the middle as her chest rose and fell regularly, deeply, as if only sleeping now. Gently, Ransom pulled Mel into his arms, cradling her close. For the first time in his life, he sat without the limitless force to wield but felt more powerful now than ever before. Finally, with love, he was able to vanquish evil while saving the innocent. Stroking a smooth olive cheek, he whispered, "I love you."

Still for one heartbeat, then two, her lips finally parted ever so slightly. "You better," she answered as eyes fluttered open slowly, looking up into the steel blue of her deliverer. "If my life is going to be in this much danger just from loving you, it better be worth it."

Ransom smiled. "No more danger, Mel. I promise."

"But what about your father? Or the man that pretended to be so?" She looked around, nervous and confused, eyes landing on Audrei. "Ransom! You have a sister!"

Audrei smiled sweetly, her round face lighting with joy. "We met," she said simply.

"Draven's long gone. Mel, I'm free. You saved me." Ransom chuckled, his easy demeanor returning.

Brown eyes locked on blue. "I'll be expecting a reward. In the meantime, we have so much to discuss."

Ransom looked from Mel to Audrei. "Luckily we have a lifetime to do so."

He set his love down in the grass before standing tall, then bent to help her up, holding firm until Mel retained balance. Audrei rose as well, straightening her skirts.

Once steady enough, Mel surveyed her own dress. "Oh my, such a waste. I loved this dress. Now it's riddled with holes."

"Speaking of holes." Ransom swept the dagger up quickly, vaguely noting the round locket door ajar. "I can't believe you stabbed me," he exclaimed good-naturedly, proffering the knife.

Looking up from her dress, Mel spied the dagger resting on top of the red silk, still wrapped around his damaged hand. "Well, it didn't seem fair that I was the only one getting hurt." Though her words were defensive, she lifted the knife and carefully caressed the wounded hand in apology, delicate fingers brushing against his palm, sliding over the silk.

"Don't worry," Ransom said good-naturedly again. "I'm tougher than I look."

"That's good. I'd hate to see you lose your edge now. Especially if you're going to be a prince." Mel laughed softly. She kept hold of his hand and turned to the young princess. "Ransom, meet Audrei."

"It's a pleasure to meet you, officially," he said, a smile spreading across the strong jaw, his signature dimple making an appearance.

Overcome, Audrei stepped forward quickly, shedding all proprieties, and threw her arms around Ransom in a long overdue embrace.

One hand wrapped around his sister, and the other pulled Mel into the group. Mel held the dagger close to her chest protectively and leaned into the warmth. The moment Imelda lay her hand on Audrei's arm, the speck inside ignited with a brightness of one hundred stars. Beams burst through the small opening in the locket door, illuminating everything around. Audrei's round eyes magnified in surprise as Ransom met Imelda's gaze. Together they laughed, knowing their search for home was finally over.

ABOUT THE AUTHOR

Calie Schmidt grew up in the middle of a large family of steps, halves, and wholes, each person adding elements and color that helped shape her outlook on life. She received the love of reading and writing from her mother. Now grown with a family of her own, Calie hopes to pass that same love to her five children. Her goal is to teach them, and any others, about the beauties in life through the art of poetry and storytelling. Her motto is "feel the Spirit, write what I know, hope to inspire." For more information, go to www.calieschmidt.com.

Scan to visit

www.calieschmidt.com